LAST REVIVAL IN PUCKERBRUSH

PUCKERBRUSH SERIES

C. DEANNE ROWE

Last Revival In Puckerbrush

Puckerbrush Series

Published by C. Deanne Rowe

www.cdeannerowe.com

Cover Art by Rebecca K. Sterling

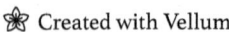 Created with Vellum

DEDICATION

For every reader who journeyed to Puckerbrush and stayed awhile, thank you for embracing these characters as your own. Your support has made this series unforgettable.

1

The faint hum of the overhead fluorescent lights was the only sound in the quiet library. Dr. Elizabeth Harper, Beth to her friends and family, sat hunched over a weathered notebook, its pages yellowed and brittle from age. She leaned closer, careful not to disturb the fragile paper as her eyes scanned the fading ink. The name appeared again, scrawled in an uneven hand that betrayed the writer's haste.

Edward Dalton

She traced the letters with her fingers, imagining the man behind the name. The traveling evangelist known for fiery sermons and crowds that swelled with fervor, yet there was always something more whispered beneath the surface. His legend spread far beyond the small towns where he had preached. Some hailed him as a prophet, others a conman.

She sat back. Her brow furrowed. The last entry was dated just days before his disappearance. With no explanation, Edward Dalton had simply vanished after one final revival meeting, leaving behind more questions than answers.

As a historian, she had learned to sift through rumor and myth, separating fact from the folklore that inevitably built up around men like Dalton. Her research was meticulous, her passion for finding the truth unrelenting. This case, however, seemed to pull her in deeper than usual. Dalton's trail was personal, and she had a secret desire for answers. Also, her new client's request was filled with a sense of urgency she couldn't ignore.

The soft chime of a bell over the library door startled her as she reached for her notebook. She looked up as a man stepped inside. His dark hair was neatly combed, and he carried himself with the tentative confidence of someone eager for answers but unsure of what they'd be.

"Dr. Harper?" he asked, approaching her table.

"Thomas?" she replied, standing and extending a hand. "Thomas Everett?"

He nodded, shaking her hand firmly. "Thank you for agreeing to meet with me. I'm sorry for the short notice, but I didn't want to waste any more time."

Beth gestured to the seat across from her. "Please, have a seat. I've been looking over the materials you sent me. I have to say, Edward Dalton's story is...complicated."

Thomas gave a tight smile, the kind that didn't quite reach his eyes. "That's one way of putting it. My family always told stories about him, about how he brought people to God, how he was a great man of faith. But..." He hesitated, his fingers tapping nervously on the edge of the table. "I've been finding things that don't match up. Letters, old records. It seems like there's more to him than the family legend."

She was already familiar with the discrepancy between public personas and hidden lives. "I've read some of those letters. It appears Edward Dalton was good at leaving pieces of himself behind, but not enough to paint a full picture. I'm curious. What do you hope to find?"

Thomas sighed, running a hand through his hair and answering in a strained voice, "Honestly? I don't know. I just need to know who he really was. The family built him up to be a saint, but if there's more to the story, I can't let it stay buried."

This was more than a research project for him. This was personal. She nodded slowly. "The last record I found puts Dalton around Puckerbrush. Have you heard of it?"

Thomas shook his head. "No. Is it a stop on his revival trail?"

"Yes," she said, flipping through her notes. "It's a small town, but it's where his trail goes cold. He and all the tithes collected during the trip disappeared after a revival there. No record of him leaving, no mention of him after that night. If we're going to find any answers, that's where we need to start."

Thomas leaned forward. His eyes suddenly sharp with interest. "Puckerbrush...what do you think happened to him and the money?"

Beth tapped her pen thoughtfully. "That's what we need to figure out. People don't just disappear, not without leaving something behind. And with Edward Dalton's history of...let's say questionable behavior, I suspect the truth is far from simple."

"Then Puckerbrush it is," Thomas said with resolve, breaking her focus. His eyes were intense, desperate for answers.

She gave him a sharp look. She could feel the weight of what lay ahead. "Puckerbrush holds more than you know, Thomas. We might not like what we find."

2

Constantine Thornton exhaled a long breath as she pulled her car into the cracked asphalt lot of the Puckerbrush Motel. It looked exactly as she remembered. A long, single-story building, weathered by time and the elements, with a neon sign that flickered faintly in the gathering dusk. The last time she'd been here, Dave was with her.

A pang of sadness hit her as she turned off the engine and let the silence settle over her. Things had seemed so different then. Christmas lights had twinkled from the eaves, and she was hopeful, full of plans for the future. She was happy with Dave, convinced they were building something together.

But that was months ago. Before the long stretches of silence, before his job started taking him farther away. Before it became clear that they were living separate lives.

Now, she was back in Puckerbrush. Alone.

She parked the car near the entrance and rubbed her hands over the steering wheel, trying to push away the feeling in her chest. She had told herself this trip was just a quick getaway, a place to find some peace after the breakup. But returning to Puckerbrush, seeing the motel, the streets. It brought everything back, not just memories of Dave, but of her family's history. The things she thought she'd left behind.

The familiar clanging of the motel bell brought a smile to her face as she pushed open the front door. Berta, the motel's owner, now Constantine's friend since previous stays, appeared at the front desk, her face lighting up in recognition.

"Well, look what the cat dragged in!" Berta said, stepping out from behind the counter with her arms outstretched. "I didn't expect to see you back for a while."

Constantine managed a small smile, grateful for the warmth in Berta's greeting. "Yeah, neither did I," she said, accepting the hug.

"You here for long?" Berta asked, giving her a once-over with a concerned look.

Constantine chuckled softly. "Just taking a break. Needed a place to think."

Berta nodded knowingly. "Well, you've come to the right place for that. Not much goes on around here that'll disturb your thoughts. Would you like the same room as before?"

"That would be great," Constantine said, the weight of the day already easing just being back in a familiar place where she knew she had support.

"Good." Berta slid the key to room eight across the desk. "You get settled in, then come by the office if you need anything. I've still got that stash of cookies if you're feeling snacky." She winked. "Oh, and don't worry. I'll let everyone I talk with know you're back in town. You know how folks around here love to stay updated," she added with a grin, her eyes twinkling.

Constantine laughed, a genuine one this time, as she walked out the door to her car. She grabbed her bag and made her way to her room. Everything looked the same, yet nothing felt the same. She opened the door and took in the modest room, the simple bed, and the old dresser. It was far from luxurious, but it was comforting.

As she set her suitcase down, her phone buzzed in her pocket. A quick glance showed it was another email from her publisher, probably about the edits for her latest book. The readers of her first book about finding her great-great-uncle Eldon had so many questions that she decided to answer them by writing a second. She ignored the email for now. Work could wait.

What she couldn't ignore were the memories that flooded her mind. Memories of her great-grandmother, Constantine Bradley Thornton, of Eldon's journals. She had written about it all, shared the stories with the world, but somehow, it still seemed there were more layers to uncover. More secrets buried in the dusty corners of Pucker-brush. There was more waiting for her here. That's why she felt drawn to return for a visit, even if it was a short one.

And with the name of Edward Dalton hanging in the back of her mind, Constantine had the unsettling feeling that this visit would bring more than peace and quiet. There were still ghosts here. Ghosts she wasn't sure she was ready to face.

3

The road stretched ahead, winding lazily through the countryside as the last hues of sunlight faded behind the hills. Dr. Elizabeth Harper glanced at the weathered sign on the roadside: *Puckerbrush—10 miles.* Her fingers tightened on the steering wheel, anticipation buzzing in her chest.

"We're almost there," she said, gently nudging the arm of her passenger, Thomas Everett.

He stirred.

With a soft tone, she said, "It's been a long day. Leaving early for the drive...I'm surprised you lasted this long."

He stretched, stifling a yawn. "I should've stayed awake to keep you company. How long have we been driving?"

Beth glanced at the dashboard clock. "A little over four hours, but we're close now. The motel isn't far." She gestured to the GPS on the dashboard. "I made reservations for us at The Puckerbrush Motel. Apparently, it's the only place in town to stay."

Thomas gave a sidelong glance, one brow lifted in silent question. "Sounds charming."

Beth chuckled. "I've stayed in worse places during research trips. If nothing else, it'll give us a feel for the town."

They fell quiet, the rhythmic hum of the tires on the asphalt filling the silence. Thomas gazed out at the scenery. "Do you believe we'll find anything concrete about Edward Dalton here?"

She considered his question, her brow furrowing slightly. "It's hard to say. Puckerbrush is where his trail goes cold, but if we're lucky, someone or something here might help us piece together what happened. Small towns like this don't forget their stories easily."

He nodded. "I just hope we're not chasing ghosts."

Her lips twitched into a faint smile. "Aren't we?"

The lights of the town came into view, scattered like faint stars against the deepening twilight. Puckerbrush seemed to materialize from the shadows, its modest skyline a mix of old storefronts and cozy homes nestled under the silhouette of surrounding fields.

The car slowed as they approached the town limits, and the subdued but unmistakable charm of the Puckerbrush Motel appeared on the right, its flickering neon sign casting a dull red glow over the cracked asphalt parking lot. Beth pulled in and parked near the entrance.

Thomas stepped out of the car, stretching as he surveyed their surroundings. "Well, it's...quaint."

She smirked. "Let's just hope the beds are comfortable and there's a decent place to eat."

They grabbed their bags and entered the motel's small office. The faint chime of a bell announced their arrival, and a cheerful woman in her sixties appeared from behind the counter. Her name tag read Berta, and her warm smile was immediate.

"Evening, folks," she said, adjusting her glasses. "You must be the Harpers."

Beth returned the smile. "Close. Dr. Elizabeth Harper and Thomas Everett. I made the reservation earlier."

Her nails painted a cheerful shade of red. Berta tapped a few keys on an old computer. "Ah, here you are. Rooms two and three, right next to each other." She handed them their keys, her gaze curious but kind. "You just visiting, or here on business?"

"A bit of both," Beth replied. "Research, mostly."

Berta's brows arched slightly, but she didn't pry. "Well, welcome to Puckerbrush. If you need anything, just holler. The Puckerbrush Café is just down Main Street. You'll enjoy their food."

"Thank you," Beth said, taking the keys. "We appreciate it."

They stepped back into the cool night air, the faint scent of fields and wood smoke drifting on the breeze. As they settled into their respective rooms, the weight of their journey seemed to hang in the air. A silent acknowledgment that their search was just beginning.

Beth placed her notebook on the small desk, flipping through her carefully compiled notes. Edward Dalton's name stared back at her, underlined and circled in the margins. She tapped her pen thoughtfully.

Somewhere in this quiet town lay the answers they sought. The question was whether they were ready to uncover them.

4

The Puckerbrush Museum stood quiet and unassuming, its red brick exterior blending seamlessly with the charm of the small town. Constantine paused outside the door, taking a moment to steady herself. It had been a whirlwind decision to return, and now that she was here, she wasn't sure what she expected to find. The museum loomed before her, a familiar marker of her first visit to Puckerbrush. A visit she hadn't realized would leave such a lasting imprint.

Her first time here felt like a lifetime ago, though it had only been a little over a year. Abigail brought her to this very place, sharing pieces of Eldon's life, her great-great-uncle who had once been the missing thread in her family's story. Those memories were vivid, as was the weight of the mystery she and Abigail had worked to unravel. Now, with her life in pieces, Constantine found herself back, seeking something she couldn't quite name.

As she got closer to the museum, she thought of Berta, the unofficial town crier. Abigail was likely the first person she'd told that Constantine was back in town. Constantine braced herself for a warm but knowing welcome.

The museum was quiet except for the faint creak of the wooden floorboards beneath her shoes. The air carried a faint mustiness, mingled with the smell of polished wood and aged paper. Constantine's footsteps echoed softly as she wandered through the gallery, her gaze brushing over the familiar exhibits.

Near the back of the museum, Abigail stood by an exhibit featuring black-and-white photographs of the town's earliest days. Her auburn hair was pulled back, and she was focused on jotting notes on a clipboard, lost in thought. Constantine lingered in the shadows, the sight stirring a sense of comfort and trepidation.

Finally, she cleared her throat. "Abigail."

Turning, Abigail's expression shifted from surprise to something harder to read. "Constantine," she said, setting down the clipboard. "I didn't know you were in town."

"I decided to take a spur-of-the-moment trip," Constantine said, managing a smile as Abigail set down the clipboard and closed the distance between them.

Abigail pulled her into a warm hug, grounding Constantine like she hadn't expected. "Are you just visiting, or is this a work trip?"

"Just visiting," Constantine replied as the hug ended.

"It's so good to see you," Abigail said, pulling back with a smile. "Did Dave come with you?"

The question struck like a bell, reverberating in the quiet room. Constantine's smile faltered, and her gaze dropped to the polished wood floor. "Dave and I...we're not together anymore."

Abigail's brow furrowed, her voice gentle. "I'm sorry, Constantine. What happened?"

She shrugged, her fingers curling around the strap of her purse. "It's complicated. I guess we just stopped agreeing. He traveled so much. We hardly ever saw each other. I needed some time to think, and he needed...something else."

Abigail's voice softened, carrying the kindness Constantine had always admired. "That must have been hard."

"It was," Constantine admitted. "Still is. That's part of why I came back. I needed to clear my head, and Puckerbrush seemed like the right place to do that."

Abigail nodded knowingly. "Puckerbrush has a way of giving you space to think. You'll have plenty of people glad to see you. Me included."

Her lips curved into a small, bittersweet smile. "Thanks, Abigail. I wasn't sure how this would feel coming back. But seeing you here...it helps."

Abigail placed a hand on her shoulder, her gaze searching Constantine's face. "You don't have to go through this alone. You know that, right? If you ever need to talk, or even just sit quietly with someone, I'm here."

Constantine blinked quickly, willing away a sting of tears. "I know. And I appreciate it and your friendship."

"Good," Abigail said. "Now, are you staying long? Or is this just a quick trip?"

"I'm not sure yet," Constantine admitted. "But I thought I'd start by stopping here and then heading to the café for lunch. It feels like the right thing to do. I got in yesterday and didn't have the chance to let anyone but Berta know I was in town."

Laughing, Abigail crossed her arms. "And she didn't tell me? She's going to hear about this later."

"It was late when I got in," Constantine said. "I'm sure she didn't want to risk waking you or the kids. How are they, by the way?"

"They are growing so fast." Abigail's face softened further with unmistakable pride. "I can't wait for you to see them. They will be thrilled you're here."

"And Matthew?" Constantine asked, genuinely curious.

"He's really good," Abigail said, glancing at the time on her phone. "He's probably about ready to have lunch at the café. Say hello to him, John, and Emily. They'd love to know you're here."

"I will," she said, the idea sparking a faint sense of anticipation. "Want to join me? We'll make it a reunion party."

Abigail laughed, a regretful shake of her head accompanying the sound. "I wish I could, but Opal's sick today. I promised her I would finish a project she's been working on, and I need to wrap it up before it's time to pick the kids up from Jeanne's. But you'll have to have dinner with us while you're here."

"I'll plan on it." Constantine's smile grew a little easier. "Right now, I think I'll head to the café."

"I'm sure everyone will be glad to see you. Enjoy yourself." Abigail hugged her again, a gesture filled with quiet affection. "It's good to see you."

"You, too," Constantine said. They made their way to the front door, and as they stepped outside, Abigail added with a grin, "And have a piece of Martha's apple pie for me."

Constantine laughed. "I'll do my best."

As Abigail waved her off, Constantine felt a flicker of warmth, the kind she hadn't realized she needed until now. Puckerbrush still had a way of making her feel good, even when life felt anything but.

5

The Puckerbrush Café bustled softly, the sound of clinking dishes and murmured conversations blending in the background. Dr. Elizabeth Harper and Thomas Everett sat at a corner table, their notebooks spread between half-eaten plates of sandwiches and steaming coffee mugs.

Thomas glanced around, taking in the homey décor, the walls lined with old photographs of Puckerbrush, jars of wildflowers on every table, and the chalkboard menu listing the day's specials in neat handwriting. "Cozy place," he remarked.

Beth nodded absently. Her eyes were fixed on the café counter, where a familiar figure moved efficiently. "Very."

Thomas followed her gaze. "That's Emily, isn't it? I thought I recognized her when she waited on us earlier."

Beth didn't answer immediately. Instead, she closed her notebook and took another sip of coffee. "It is. And if she's anything like she was on *Tracing Your Heritage*, this conversation will be...interesting."

Behind the counter, Emily moved with practiced ease. But there was something in the set of her shoulders, the faint tension in her movements, that suggested she'd already noticed the strangers.

"Should we call her over?" Thomas asked.

Beth shook her head. "No need. She's already coming."

Sure enough, Emily approached a moment later, coffeepot in hand and a polite smile on her face. "How are you folks doing? Need a refill?"

"Please," Beth said, offering her cup.

She filled it carefully before turning her attention to Thomas. "And you?"

"I'm good, thanks," he said, setting his mug down.

Emily lingered, her smile still in place. "You two aren't from around here, are you?"

"We're not," Beth replied smoothly. "I'm Dr. Elizabeth Harper, and this is Thomas Everett. I'm a historian, here doing research with Thomas concerning his family."

Emily's smile didn't waver, but her eyes sharpened ever so slightly. "Research, huh? Puckerbrush isn't exactly a hotspot for historians."

"Maybe it should be," Beth said. "There's a lot of history here. Take Edward Dalton, for example."

The smile froze on Emily's face.

"We're tracing his revival trail," Beth continued. "It led us here."

Emily's grip on the coffeepot tightened slightly before she set it on the table. "Edward Dalton? That's...an old name. What brought you to him?"

Beth's gaze was steady. "You did, actually."

Emily blinked. "Me?"

Beth nodded. "Your episode of *Tracing Your Heritage*. It was a beautiful story of how you, Matthew Thompson, and Samuel Piper reconnected. But it wasn't just the family reunion that caught my attention."

Emily's expression grew wary. "What did?"

"The part about Edward Dalton," Beth said. "Your ancestor. A man whose legacy seems to cast a long shadow, even now."

Emily hesitated, her hands fidgeting with the edge of her apron. "That was a long time ago. I don't know much about him, honestly."

Leaning back slightly, Beth's tone was casual, but her eyes were sharp. "Maybe not. But you're his relative, and you live in the town where his trail goes cold. That seems...important."

Emily glanced toward the door, where a new customer entered. She exhaled, her smile returning, though it lacked its earlier warmth. "I don't know what you're hoping to find, Dr. Harper, but people around here don't talk much about the revivals. It's just old history."

"Old history has a way of sticking around," Beth said, her voice calm but insistent.

Stepping back slightly, Emily picked up the coffeepot. "If you'll excuse me, I need to check on the other tables."

"Of course," Beth said, watching Emily quickly walk away.

Thomas waited until she was out of earshot before leaning forward. "That went well."

Beth smirked faintly. "She knows something. Whether she's willing to share is another matter."

6

The aroma of freshly brewed coffee and freshly baked pastry greeted Constantine. She paused, taking in the familiar scene. The well-worn wooden tables, the comforting hum of quiet conversation, and the soft strains of music playing from the radio in the corner.

Emily broke into a wide grin. "Well, if it isn't Constantine Thornton!" she exclaimed, wiping her hands on her apron as she came around the counter. "Welcome back!"

John walked through the door leading to the kitchen, his sleeves rolled up and a dish towel slung over his shoulder. "It's good to see you, Constantine," he said, his voice carrying the weight of genuine affection.

Seated at the end of the counter with a steaming mug of coffee, Matthew raised his cup in greeting. "Constantine. What brings you back to Puckerbrush?"

She couldn't help but smile, her heart lifting at the sight of their familiar faces. "It's good to see all of you. I would have shown up sooner if I had known I'd get such a warm welcome."

"You should know better," Emily said, pulling her into a quick hug. "Once Puckerbrush claims you, there's no escaping it."

"Especially when Emily's cinnamon rolls are involved," Matthew quipped, earning a quick eye roll from Emily.

Constantine's gaze drifted to the far corner of the café where two people she didn't recognize sat at a small table, deep in conversation. The woman was gesturing animatedly as she jotted in a notebook. The man nodded, his expression a mix of curiosity and determination. The two were noticeably engrossed in their discussion.

Constantine's gaze lingered on the pair. There was something about them that piqued her curiosity. With her sharp features and an air of focused intensity, the woman seemed like someone used to asking questions and finding answers. On the other hand, the man had a quieter demeanor, his movements deliberate, his attention unwavering.

"New faces?" she asked, tilting her head toward the corner table.

Emily glanced over her shoulder, following Constantine's gaze. "Oh, that's Dr. Harper and her friend. They're staying at the motel. Been in town since last night."

"Dr. Harper?" Constantine repeated, the name unfamiliar.

"She's a historian," Emily said, lowering her voice just enough to make it seem like she was sharing a secret. "She's researching Edward Dalton."

Constantine froze, the name striking her like an icy wind. "Edward Dalton?" she repeated, her voice barely above a whisper.

Emily nodded. "Yeah, apparently, he held his last revival here. They've been asking questions around town, trying to piece together what happened to him."

Constantine's heart quickened at memories of Abigail and Matthew allowing her to read the entry in her great-great-uncle Eldon's journal. She learned the truth about Edward Dalton. How his fiery sermons concealed a darker side, how his charm and charisma led to tragedy. How Eldon had taken justice into his own hands after the death of his beloved daughter.

"Constantine?" Emily's voice pulled her back to the present. "You okay? You look like you've seen a ghost."

Forcing herself to shake off the shock, she managed a weak smile. "I'm fine," she blurted. "Just surprised."

"Well, historians dig up all kinds of things, don't they?" Emily replied, oblivious to the storm brewing in Constantine's mind. "They seem harmless enough, though. Just here for research," she said before entering the kitchen.

Nodding, Constantine's gaze flicked back to the corner table. The two strangers didn't seem dangerous, but their presence unsettled her. What if they uncovered the truth? What if they found out what Eldon had done? The thought sent a chill down her spine. She had left the truth out of her book to keep the secret between family.

Matthew's voice from behind her broke her contemplation. "You're thinking about Edward Dalton, aren't you?"

She turned to glance at him, startled by his perceptiveness. "How could I not? They're here to dig up his story."

Matthew's eyes narrowed as he looked at their table. "Of all the things to poke around in, they had to pick him."

"They don't know what they're walking into," Constantine murmured, almost to herself.

"Maybe not, but it won't take much for them to start asking the wrong people the right questions," Matthew said, his voice low but firm. "And if that happens…"

She exhaled shakily. "We'd have to deal with the fallout."

Matthew nodded grimly. "Abigail and I always knew this would catch up to us someday. We told you because it felt like the right thing to do since you were family, but…" He paused, shaking his head. "The truth coming out now, after all these years?"

Constantine frowned, her mind racing. "But if they're just here for research, maybe they won't dig that deep."

Matthew gave her a pointed look. "They wouldn't have come all the way to Puckerbrush if they didn't think there was something worth finding. Dr. Elizabeth Harper doesn't look like the type to stop at the surface."

Glancing back at the corner table, her unease grew. "What do we do?" She knew the truth they were searching for, yet the words stayed inside her. If she spoke them aloud, she would betray the people she now knew as family. Eldon's choices were complicated, but they were her family's burdens, and no one else needed to know.

"For now?" Matthew took a breath to steady himself. "We keep an eye on them. And if they start sniffing around where they shouldn't, we'll figure out what comes next. Me, you, Abigail, and Eldon are the only ones who know the truth."

Constantine nodded again, forcing a small smile as she slid onto a stool at the counter. But her thoughts were already racing. She'd come back to Puckerbrush for peace, to escape her own ghosts. Instead, it seemed the town's ghosts were stirring again, and this time, they weren't content to stay hidden.

7

Constantine hadn't planned on leaving the café so soon. But the presence of the two strangers, coupled with Matthew's warning, left her uneasy. The name Edward Dalton lingered in her mind like an unwelcome ghost. She needed to talk to Abigail.

Crossing the street, she entered the Puckerbrush Museum. The faint scent of freshly potted flowers drifted through the open door. The quiet inside was almost oppressive, wrapping around her like the weight of the secrets she, Abigail, and Matthew shared.

"Abigail?" she called out, her voice echoing in the quiet space.

"In the back!" came the familiar reply.

Constantine found her in the back, at a table surrounded by stacks of papers and a half-empty teacup. A notebook lay open in front of her. She was jotting something down when Constantine stepped into the room. Abigail glanced up, her face brightening.

"Back already?" She set her pen down, brushing a loose strand of hair behind her ear. "I thought you were staying at the café for lunch."

Placing the paper bag on the table, Constantine slid into the chair across from her. "Change of plans. Something came up."

Abigail lifted an eyebrow. "What kind of something?"

Leaning forward, she said, "A historian and her friend are in town. They're asking questions about Edward Dalton. Emily said they're here to research his revivals."

Abigail's expression shifted instantly, her shoulders stiffened, and her eyes narrowed. "Dalton?" she repeated, the words heavy with unspoken weight.

Constantine nodded. "Matthew believes they could cause trouble if they dig too deep. He suggested we keep an eye on them, but I don't know. It feels like we need to know more about who we're dealing with first."

Sitting back in her chair, Abigail's gaze sharpened. "Did you get their names?"

"Dr. Elizabeth Harper and Thomas Everett," Constantine replied. "Do you know them?"

"Not off the top of my head," Abigail admitted, reaching for her phone. "Let's see what the internet has to say about Dr. Harper."

Constantine watched as she typed quickly, her fingers tapping the screen with practiced efficiency. After a moment of scrolling, Abigail's brows knit together.

"Here we go," she said, her voice turning serious. "Dr. Elizabeth Harper, PhD. Historian and author, specializes in uncovering the hidden stories. Specifically, ones that small towns would rather keep buried." She clicked on a link, scanned the page, and glanced up, her lips pressing into a thin line. "Her last book was about a church scandal. Missing funds, destroyed reputations...she doesn't pull any punches."

Constantine's stomach churned. "Great. Just what we need."

Abigail kept reading, "She's thorough. And she's not afraid to stir the pot. If she's here, she already believes there's a story."

Constantine sank back into her chair. "That's exactly what we don't need. If she pulls at the wrong threads..."

"She'll unravel everything," Abigail finished grimly. She placed her phone face down on the table, her expression thoughtful. "We need to stay ahead of this. At the very least, we need to know for sure what she's after."

Her voice quiet, Constantine nodded. "I left this part of the story out of my book. After you and Matthew told me the truth about what happened...I just couldn't write it. I wanted to protect Eldon and our family."

Her fingers tracing the rim of her teacup, Abigail hesitated. "We wait. We listen. For now, it's all we can do. If we draw too much attention, we might make things worse."

The knot in Constantine's stomach tightened. "I came back to clear my head, not walk into another mystery."

Abigail gave her a small, knowing smile. "Puckerbrush has a way of stirring things up when you least expect it."

Constantine released a slow breath. "I don't know if I'm ready for this."

Reaching across the table, Abigail's hand rested over hers. "No one ever is. But you're not alone in this. We'll figure it out together."

The faint trill of a bird outside the window filled the silence between them. Abigail's grip on Constantine's hand tightened briefly before she let go and sat back.

"I'll keep an ear out around town," Abigail said. "Let me know if you see or hear anything else."

"I will." A small smile tugged at the corner of Constantine's mouth as she opened the brown sack and removed two pieces of apple pie and sandwiches. "What if we eat the lunch I brought and talk about something else for a while?"

Abigail chuckled, her shoulders visibly relaxing. "I thought you'd never ask."

As the scent of cinnamon and warm apples filled the room, Constantine felt slightly better. But even as the two women settled into a lighter conversation, she couldn't shake the lingering unease. Puckerbrush might be quiet on the surface, but beneath the lilacs and sunlight, old shadows waited for the right moment to rise.

8

"Thanks for everything, Emily," Matthew placed a twenty-dollar bill on the counter and stood from his stool, grasping his hat with one hand.

Emily wiped her hands on her apron and smiled. "You're welcome. Same time tomorrow?"

Matthew nodded, his gaze flickering toward the corner of the café. Dr. Harper and Thomas Everett were seated there, hunched over notebooks and papers spread across the table like conspirators. "I think I'll go introduce myself to our visitors."

Emily followed his gaze, her smile dimming slightly. "They said they watched our episode of *Tracing Your Heritage*."

"Thanks." His sheriff's badge caught the sunlight streaming through the café window as he adjusted his belt then slipped his hat back on his head.

He crossed the room with a deliberate stride, his boots scuffing lightly against the worn wooden floor. The woman looked up first, her sharp, analytical eyes meeting his. The man followed, a hint of uncertainty flickering across his face.

"Sheriff Matthew Thompson." He offered his hand, his tone polite but firm. "I understand you're in town looking for information about Edward Dalton."

The woman extended her hand with a confident smile. "Dr. Elizabeth Harper. And yes, we are. Thank you for coming over." She gestured toward Thomas. "This is Thomas Everett. He's a relative of Edward Dalton, and I'm helping him trace his family's history. We're hoping to find some answers and closure, if we're lucky."

Matthew pulled a chair from the nearest table and sat down. "You believe you're going to find that here in Puckerbrush?"

"I caught the episode of *Tracing Your Heritage,* where you, Emily, and Samuel Piper talked about your connection to Edward Dalton."

"What makes you think Emily, Piper, or I would know anything more than what we said on *Tracing Your Heritage*? That episode covered everything we've got on Dalton."

Dr. Harper's gaze didn't waver. "We've traced Dalton's revival trail, Sheriff, and all signs point to Puckerbrush as the last place he was seen. A man like him doesn't just vanish without leaving something behind. Someone here must know more than they're saying."

Matthew leaned back slightly, resting one arm on the back of his chair. His eyes locked on Thomas. "And you think you'll find that someone in Puckerbrush?"

"Don't you?" Her question hung in the air, her calm persistence a direct challenge.

Matthew allowed a small smile to play at the corner of his lips. "I can send you across the street to our town museum. My wife, Abigail, runs it. She's the keeper of our history, and if there's anything on Dalton, it'll be there."

Dr. Harper closed her notebook with a snap, her smile returning. "I'd love to meet your wife and see what the museum offers. We were about to finish up here, anyway."

Matthew rose from this chair, setting it back in place. "Abigail will show you what we've got. Let me be clear, Puckerbrush is a friendly town, but folks here value their privacy. I wouldn't want to hear that anyone's been upset by your questions. Edward Dalton may have held his last revival here, but he also caused a lot of pain."

Thomas shifted in his seat, glancing at Dr. Harper. She nodded. Her tone was measured. "We'll be careful, Sheriff. I promise."

"I hope so." Matthew tipped his hat slightly. "It was nice meeting you both. I'm sure we'll cross paths again before you leave."

"Likewise, Sheriff." Her tone was light, but her eyes were already calculating their next steps.

Matthew exited the café, the door jingling softly behind him. As soon as he was out of sight, he pulled his phone from his pocket and dialed Abigail.

"Hi," she answered, her voice warm. "Is everything okay?"

"I just met our out-of-town historian," Matthew said, his voice low. "Dr. Elizabeth Harper and Thomas Everett. They're on their way to see you."

"Dalton?" Abigail asked, a note of tension creeping into her tone.

"Yep. They're looking for answers. I know you'll handle them."

She exhaled audibly. "Thanks for the heads-up. Love you."

"Love you too. See you at home later." Matthew ended the call, sliding his phone into his pocket.

Climbing into his patrol car, he glanced back through the café's front window. Dr. Harper and Thomas were standing now, gathering their things and exchanging a few words before heading toward the door. He started the engine, but his eyes remained on them as they stepped onto the sidewalk and crossed the street to the Puckerbrush Museum.

The secrets of Puckerbrush were buried deep, and Matthew knew better than anyone that some truths were better left unfound. However, historians like Elizabeth Harper didn't stop until they had answers. And answers, in Puckerbrush, always came with a cost.

9

A bigail Thompson worked methodically at her desk inside the museum, organizing a new exhibit featuring early photographs of Puckerbrush's founders.

The chime of the front door broke the stillness, drawing her attention. She glanced up to see two people stepping inside. Dr. Elizabeth Harper and Thomas Everett, she presumed. They scanned the room with the kind of intensity Abigail had learned to recognize. They were people on a mission, hoping to unearth something long buried.

Abigail rose from her desk, her expression polite but guarded. "Good afternoon. Can I help you?"

"Mrs. Thompson?" the woman asked, stepping forward with a confident smile. "I'm Dr. Elizabeth Harper, and this is Thomas Everett. We're researching Edward Dalton. Your husband mentioned you might help us."

Abigail's stomach tightened, though she maintained her composure. She extended her hand. "Yes, Matthew told me you'd be stopping by. Please, have a seat."

They settled into the chairs across from her desk, their notebooks already open. Abigail returned to her seat, folding her hands in front of her. She met Dr. Harper's gaze directly, her expression calm but unreadable.

"So," Abigail said, "you're researching Edward Dalton. Is that what brings you to Puckerbrush, Dr. Harper?"

"Please, call me Beth," she replied, leaning forward slightly. "We've been following his revival trail across Texas, and the trail ends here. We're hoping to find out what happened to him after his last revival."

Abigail's lips curved into a faint smile, though her pulse quickened. "That's a challenging question. Edward Dalton's story is old, and most people in town don't know much about him."

"But you have records, don't you?" Thomas asked, his tone quieter but no less eager. "Flyers, newspapers, anything from the time?"

"We do," Abigail replied, her tone even. "The museum keeps a collection of documents from that era, including a few things from the revival. But I should warn you, there's not much. Dalton didn't leave a large footprint here."

Beth's sharp gaze narrowed slightly. "A man like Edward Dalton doesn't just vanish without leaving something behind. Surely someone here knows more about what happened to him."

Abigail hesitated, choosing her words carefully. "Sometimes people don't want to remember. And sometimes, there's simply nothing left to tell."

Tilting her head, Beth studied her. "Do you believe that's the case here?"

Abigail stood, moving toward a filing cabinet along the back wall. "I believe history is often incomplete. But you're welcome to look through what we have." She pulled out a folder of documents, flyers, newspaper clippings, and a few grainy photographs and set them on the desk.

Beth and Thomas leaned in immediately, their pens poised. Abigail watched them, her mind racing. Only she, Matthew, and Constantine knew the truth about Dalton. The truth that was recorded in Eldon's journal and left for Abigail to find. Dalton hadn't vanished. He had been killed, and Eldon had buried the secret along with the man.

"How did people here feel about Dalton?" Thomas asked as he flipped through the papers. "Was he popular?"

"For some," Abigail said, keeping her tone neutral. "Others were more skeptical. Revivals like his could be...polarizing."

Beth glanced up. "What do you mean by that?"

Abigail smiled faintly, sitting back down. "Faith has a way of stirring powerful emotions. Dalton had his supporters, but not everyone saw him as a savior. Some found his methods questionable."

"That's putting it lightly," Beth muttered, jotting something in her notebook.

Abigail's gaze lingered on Beth before she spoke again. "You mentioned you're helping Thomas with his family's history. Is Edward Dalton a direct ancestor of yours?"

Thomas nodded. "My great-grandfather. My family always spoke of him as a man of faith, someone who brought people closer to God. But the more I've uncovered, the more I believe there's another side to his story."

"There usually is," Abigail said, her fingers brushing the edge of the desk. "But small towns like Puckerbrush are protective of their stories. If there's more to Dalton's past, it's likely buried deeply."

Beth's pen paused over her notebook. "Sometimes the most valuable stories are the ones people don't want to tell."

Abigail's smile didn't falter. "Perhaps. But history can be stubborn. It doesn't always give up its secrets."

The room fell quiet, the faint rustle of papers filling the silence. Abigail felt the weight of their presence. The questions they carried pressing against the fragile truth she and Matthew had worked so hard to protect.

"This is a good start," Beth said, closing her notebook. "We'd like to revisit these records later, if that's alright."

"Of course," Abigail said. "Just let me know."

Thomas hesitated, glancing at Abigail. "Do you think anyone in town might have stories passed down through their families? Something about Dalton's time here?"

Abigail shook her head slowly, her voice steady. "None that I've heard other than Emily, Matthew, and Piper. But small towns have their whispers. If you're careful, you might find someone willing to share."

Beth and Thomas stood, gathering their things. Beth extended a hand. "Thank you for your time, Mrs. Thompson. We appreciate your help."

Abigail shook her hand, walking them to the door. "You're welcome. Let me know if you need anything else."

As the door closed behind them, Abigail let out a slow breath, her shoulders stiffening. She hurried back to her desk, picked up her phone, and dialed Matthew.

"They just left," she said when he answered.

"What did you tell them?" Matthew's voice was calm but edged with concern.

"I let them look at everything we have from around the time Dalton was here in Puckerbrush," Abigail replied. "Matthew, they're determined. If we're not careful, they'll dig up more than we want them to. With Constantine in town, we might have to be very careful."

Matthew's response was firm. "We'll make sure they don't dig up anything we don't want them to."

Abigail sighed. "We need to talk with Constantine and make sure she's on board with staying quiet. I invited her over for dinner while she's in town. We'll talk to her then."

"Sounds good," Matthew said.

As she ended the call, Abigail stared out the window. Dr. Elizabeth Harper might be relentless, but she wasn't about to let her unravel the truth. Not when the cost of that truth was so steep.

Beth Harper flipped through the notebook in her lap, her precise handwriting filling its pages. She tapped her pen against the edge of the paper, her thoughts lingering on the name at the top: Samuel Piper.

The hum of the motel's air conditioner was the only sound until Thomas Everett broke the silence. "Do you think he'll even talk to us? He's a sheriff like Matthew. He's not in the habit of sharing information unless it's necessary."

Beth glanced up, her eyes narrowing slightly. "He's not *just* a sheriff. He's a descendant of Edward Dalton, just like Emily and Matthew. That makes him important. And he was on *Tracing Your Heritage*. He knows as much as they do."

Thomas crossed his arms. "Matthew and Emily barely spoke to us. Matthew was polite but distant, and Emily practically ran out of the room. What makes you think Samuel Piper will be any different?"

Beth smiled faintly. "He may see things differently. He might not be eager to talk, but he'll know how to keep emotions out of it."

Thomas tilted his head, unconvinced. "But what if he doesn't want to air the family's dirty laundry? That *Tracing Your*

Heritage episode made everything look warm and fuzzy. No way they dug into Dalton's darker side."

Beth's pen stilled as she met his gaze. "That's a risk we'll have to take. If Samuel Piper knows anything about Dalton's legacy, he might give us a lead the others didn't or won't."

Thomas sighed. "Fine. Do you at least know where to find him?"

"I called the Johnson County Sheriff's Office earlier," Beth said, closing her notebook. "Samuel Piper is their sheriff. We'll start there."

Thomas smirked. "Of course, you already called. Why am I not surprised?"

Beth grabbed her bag and stood. "Because you know me. Let's go."

AN HOUR EAST OF PUCKERBRUSH, the Johnson County Sheriff's Office was a modest brick building, its small parking lot dotted with patrol cars. Inside, the air smelled faintly of coffee and disinfectant. A receptionist greeted them with a polite smile.

"We're here to see Sheriff Piper," Beth said.

The receptionist made a quick call and gestured toward a hallway. "Second door on the left."

Samuel Piper sat behind a sturdy wooden desk, his sharp gaze immediately locking onto them as they entered. A framed photo rested on the corner of the desk, its glass catching the sunlight streaming through the blinds.

"Dr. Harper, Mr. Everett," Piper said, standing to shake their hands. "I had a feeling you'd come by. Both Emily and Matthew told me you were visiting Puckerbrush and asking questions."

Beth smiled. "Thank you for seeing us, Sheriff. I'm sure Matthew and Emily let you know we're researching Edward Dalton, and your name came up in the *Tracing Your Heritage* episode along with theirs."

Piper gestured for them to sit. "That episode stirred up a lot of interest in Dalton. What exactly are you hoping to find?"

Thomas leaned forward. "The truth. My family always talked

about Dalton like he was a saint, but the records we've found suggest a more complicated story."

Piper leaned back. His expression was unreadable. "Your family? So you're related to Edward Dalton?"

"He's my great-grandfather," Thomas explained.

"Well, complicated is one way to put Edward Dalton. He wasn't the saint some people make him out to be. His revivals brought many people to faith, but they left plenty of damage in their wake."

Beth tilted her head. "And what's your perspective? As one of his descendants?"

Piper's jaw tightened slightly. "My perspective is that Dalton's legacy is a tangle of faith, power, and manipulation. But there's more than one perspective on him."

Thomas frowned. "Are you saying there are others we should talk to?"

Piper hesitated, his fingers tapping once on the photo frame. "Martin Wright. He's a retired pastor who lives in Dallas. He and Edward Dalton were close once. Close enough that they founded a church together when they were younger. Martin stayed behind to care for the church while Dalton went out on revivals to raise funds."

Beth's pen hovered over her notebook. "So, Martin Wright would know about Dalton's early life?"

"He'd know more than most," Piper said. "And he might tell you about Joseph Wright, his adopted son. Joseph is another piece of the puzzle. A man who grew up in the shadow of Dalton's choices."

Thomas gave a sidelong glance. "Adopted son?"

Piper nodded. "You see, years ago, a young, unmarried woman named Penelope left her infant son at Martin's church. She was desperate, afraid her family would disown her because of the scandal. The baby was Dalton's, though you won't find that written down anywhere. Martin raised Joseph as his own."

Beth leaned back, processing the revelation. "And Joseph Wright is...?"

"Dalton's son. He runs a mega church in Dallas. Built his career preaching salvation and redemption, but he denies his connection to Dalton. We found out differently when a woman named Heidi Collins came to us after seeing us on *Tracing Your Heritage*. She had a son she claimed was Joseph Wright's. Of course, he denied it and even managed to pass a paternity test, showing the boy wasn't his."

Beth sat up in her chair. "How do you know that he's the father of Heidi Collins's son?"

"We ran a DNA test on the son, Peter, and he was a match with Matthew, Emily, and me. There was no doubt he was the grandson of Edward Dalton," Piper explained.

"Why hasn't anyone mentioned them before?" Beth asked. "You didn't speak of Martin or Joseph Wright on your *Tracing Your Heritage* episode."

Piper's tone cooled, a trace of steel entering his voice. "We were sent cease and desist letters preventing us from talking about it, and because it's not something the family likes to discuss. And some stories need to stay quiet for the sake of the people they touch. Penelope... she carried a lot of shame for what happened. She doesn't deserve to have her name dragged back into this."

Beth frowned slightly. "Why are you so protective of her?"

Piper's lips thinned, but he relented after a moment. "Because Penelope is my wife's grandmother. Lydia is proud of her family, and I won't see Penelope's name tarnished for choices she made when she had no good options."

"May we talk to Lydia, then?" Beth asked.

"No!" Piper exclaimed. "My wife is pregnant, and I won't have strangers upsetting her. Lydia is off limits."

Thomas caught on quickly. "We should go to Martin and Joseph instead of asking around here."

Piper's expression softened slightly. "That would be my advice. I don't know Martin Wright, and I'm not sure what kind of reception you'll receive. As for Joseph, he can decide for himself how much he wants to tell you. I wouldn't guarantee anything he says will be the truth."

Beth closed her notebook with a thoughtful nod. "Thank you, Sheriff. This gives us a lot to consider."

Piper stood. His expression was still guarded. "Be careful. Dalton's story has sharp edges, and they've cut plenty of people. Some questions might lead you to answers, but others... might just open old wounds."

11

———

S amuel Piper sat at his desk long after they left, the familiar weight of responsibility pressing down on his shoulders. The soft buzz of the office phone startled him from his thoughts, but he ignored it. His attention was focused elsewhere. On the framed photo of Lydia on his desk.

Protecting her, their unborn child, and Lydia's grandmother, Penelope, had always been his priority. He'd steered the curious strangers toward Joseph Wright, a man who could handle whatever questions they threw at him. But there was one loose end he needed to tie up.

He reached for his cellphone, searching for the contact. The line rang twice before a voice came through, steady and calm, "Matthew Thompson."

"It's Piper. Do you have a minute?"

"For you? Always," Matthew replied, a hint of curiosity in his tone. "What's on your mind?"

Piper exhaled slowly, leaning back in his chair. "Dr. Elizabeth Harper and Thomas Everett stopped by today."

There was a pause on the other end before Matthew spoke, his voice cautious. "I figured it wouldn't take long for them to get around to you."

"Well, I'm guessing you didn't tell them much," Piper said.

"Nope. Emily didn't want to talk about it, and I told them what they wanted to hear without really telling them anything. I didn't think stirring up the past would do anyone any good."

"Neither did I," Piper said. "But they're digging, and they're determined. I had to give them something. They mentioned talking with Penelope and Lydia. I nipped that in the bud quickly. I can't have them upsetting Lydia."

Matthew's tone sharpened. "What did you tell them?"

"I pointed them toward Joseph Wright and his father, Martin," Piper said, keeping his tone steady, though he knew the reaction would be immediate.

"You what?" Matthew's voice rose. "You sent them to Joseph?"

"I did," Piper said. "It was the only move that made sense."

Matthew let out a sharp breath. "Piper, you know what Joseph's like. He's not exactly a team player when it comes to this family." The cease and desist order preventing them from speaking publicly about Edward Dalton still rankled.

"I know," Piper said. "But he's a public figure. He knows how to handle himself. Penelope and Lydia don't need to be dragged into this mess. Joseph can deflect whatever they throw at him, and he won't lose any sleep over it."

Matthew's voice softened slightly. "I'm glad to hear you're protecting them."

"Of course I am," Piper said, his tone hardening. "Penelope trusted me with her story, and Lydia's been through enough without strangers dredging up the past. Now that she's pregnant, I won't have them talking to her. Joseph can handle the heat. Penelope and Lydia can't."

Matthew was quiet. "I get it. And you're right. Joseph is used to controlling the narrative, and if they're determined to find answers, he's better equipped to deal with them than anyone else."

"Exactly," Piper said. "But I wanted you to hear it from me before you got blindsided. Those two seem determined, and they'll probably head straight to Dallas."

Matthew chuckled dryly. "Let's hope Joseph doesn't lose his cool. You know how he gets when someone tries to poke holes in his story."

Piper smirked faintly. "That's his problem. Like I said, Joseph can take care of himself. What matters is keeping Penelope and Lydia out of this."

Matthew's voice turned reflective. "You're right, as usual. I should've expected you'd have a plan. You always do."

"That's part of the job," Piper replied, though his voice carried a note of weariness. "But Matthew, you, Emily, and I know Dalton's story is like a wildfire. Once it sparks, it's hard to control. Just make sure you're ready if those two come back."

"I will," Matthew said. "Thanks for the heads-up and for always looking out for us."

"Always," Piper said. "That's what family is for. Make sure you tell Emily about our call. I don't want her left out of the loop."

"I will. I'll see her tomorrow at the café. I'll make sure she knows everything we talked about. Tell Lydia that Abigail and I are looking forward to seeing you two soon. Maybe dinner."

"We'd like that. Thanks. Talk to you soon." Piper ended the call and picked up Lydia's picture from his desk. He would do everything he could to keep Harper and Everett away from her and Penelope.

12

The Dallas skyline shimmered in the early afternoon sunlight, a sharp contrast to the quiet charm of Puckerbrush. Beth Harper adjusted her glasses and checked her notes as Thomas Everett navigated the car through the crowded streets.

"This is it," Thomas said, pointing at the sprawling modern building ahead. The sleek structure, adorned with towering glass windows and a prominent white cross, stood like a monument. "Wright Way Church."

Beth raised her eyebrows, impressed despite herself. "Understated," she quipped, her voice dripping with irony.

Thomas chuckled as he parked in the visitors' lot. "Let's hope their answers are less polished than the building."

The air inside buzzed with quiet activity. The marble-floored atrium gleamed under natural light streaming through massive windows, and a faint citrus scent hung in the air. A large portrait of a man dominated one wall, his piercing gaze seemingly following them. Below his image, a plaque read: *Joseph Wright, Pastor, Wright Way Church.*

Beth glanced at it, then muttered, "He's not exactly shy, is he?"

With his gaze locked on the portrait, Thomas said, "He looks a lot like the pictures I have of my great-grandfather. I can definitely see a resemblance."

A young woman greeted them at the reception desk with a professional smile. "Welcome to Wright Way Church. How can I assist you today?"

"We're here to see Pastor Joseph Wright," Beth said, her tone polite but firm.

The receptionist's practiced expression wavered. "Do you have an appointment?"

"We don't," Thomas admitted. "But we've come a long way, and it's important."

"May I tell Pastor Wright what this is about?" the receptionist asked.

"Edward Dalton," Thomas said.

The receptionist hesitated, then picked up the phone. "Please wait here while I see if Pastor Wright is available."

Beth took a moment to survey the room, her gaze landing on a polished plaque displaying the church's mission: *Building Faith, Changing Lives, and Leading the Way to Christ.* She made a note of it before the receptionist returned.

"Pastor Wright is currently unavailable," she said, her tone apologetic. "However, Reverend Martin Wright has agreed to meet with you."

Beth and Thomas exchanged glances. "We'd be happy to speak with Reverend Wright," Beth replied.

They were escorted down a quiet hallway to a modestly furnished meeting room. Moments later, Martin Wright entered. What was left of hair that was once red, was neatly combed, and his eyes, though kind, carried years of exhaustion. He extended a wrinkled, knobby hand.

"I'm Reverend Martin Wright," he said. "I understand you wanted to talk with my son, Joseph?"

Thomas stepped forward, shaking his hand. "Thank you for

meeting with us, Reverend Wright. I'm Thomas Everett, and this is Dr. Elizabeth Harper. Sheriff Samuel Piper suggested we speak with you. We're researching Edward Dalton's legacy, and your name came up."

Martin's smile tightened as he gestured for them to sit. "Sheriff Piper? I've never had the pleasure," he muttered before sitting down. "What exactly are you hoping to learn?"

Beth didn't waste time. "We know you co-founded a church with Edward Dalton. Sheriff Piper suggested you'd have insights into his ministry, the personal impact of his choices, and what happened to him."

Martin sighed, his shoulders sagging. "It's true. Edward and I started a small church together many years ago. I stayed behind to care for the congregation while he traveled on revival tours. He had a charisma that drew crowds...but it wasn't without cost."

"What kind of cost?" Thomas asked.

Martin hesitated, his expression clouding. "Edward took what he wanted, no matter the consequences. That included trust, money, and sometimes people's lives. He left a trail of pain behind him. Leaving people to clean up after him."

Beth leaned forward. "And Joseph Wright? Were you cleaning up after Edward Dalton with him? Sheriff Piper said Joseph was Edward Dalton's son."

Martin's expression tightened slightly. "Joseph is my son in every way. He has always been a deeply private person," he said. "He's built his ministry on his own terms, and whatever Edward Dalton did, has no bearing on Joseph or our work here."

Beth tilted her head. "There have been rumors about his personal life. We've heard about a woman named Heidi Collins and her son, Peter."

The door opened abruptly, and Joseph Wright entered. His tailored suit was impeccable, his dark eyes burning with suspicion. "Reverend Wright, I'll take it from here."

Martin stood reluctantly. His expression was conflicted. "Joseph—"

"Thank you, Reverend," Joseph said, his tone curt. "I'll handle this."

As Martin left, Joseph turned to Beth and Thomas. "You've got ten minutes. Let's get to the point."

Joseph Wright stood tall, his commanding presence filling the room as he studied Beth and Thomas. His dark eyes flicked between them, sharp with suspicion but devoid of emotion.

"So," he said, his voice clipped. "What brings you here? You must have a reason for barging into my church."

Beth adjusted her glasses, keeping her tone steady. "We're here because of Edward Dalton."

Joseph blinked, the name landing heavily between them. His expression didn't falter, but there was a brief flicker of something. Surprise, perhaps. Then his features hardened. "What about Edward Dalton?"

Thomas leaned forward slightly with his hands clasped in front of him. "I'm researching my family's connection to him. Edward Dalton was my great-grandfather."

Joseph's jaw tightened subtly, but he said nothing, waiting for Thomas to continue.

"For most of my life, my family spoke about him like he was a saint," Thomas said. "But the more I've dug into his past, the more I've found cracks in that story. I'm trying to understand what really happened...to him and to the people he left behind."

Joseph's eyes narrowed slightly. "And you assume I have the answers?"

Beth chimed in, "We've talked with Sheriff Matthew Thompson and Emily Johnson in Puckerbrush. We've also talked with Sheriff Samuel Piper in Johnson County. He suggested you might have some answers. He said you're in a unique position to speak to Edward Dalton's legacy."

A cold, humorless smile tugged at Joseph's lips. "Sheriff Piper is mistaken. I know nothing about Dalton that isn't already public knowledge. My father and Edward might have started a church when they were younger, but that has nothing to do with me. Whatever story you're chasing, I'm not part of it."

Thomas didn't flinch. "Pastor Wright, you've built a ministry here. A church that even you admit began with Edward Dalton. I believe you know more than you're letting on."

"I don't," Joseph said, his tone flat. "Edward Dalton's story is his own, and I have no reason to get involved in it."

Beth pressed gently. "What about your family, then? Did Edward Dalton's choices affect them? Shape their lives in ways you might not have acknowledged?"

Joseph's expression darkened, and his voice grew colder. "My family is irrelevant to this conversation."

Thomas wasn't deterred. "I don't think they are. If we're going to understand the full picture of Edward Dalton, we need to consider everyone he impacted...including you."

Joseph's composure slipped, his hand gripping the back of the chair beside him. "This church was built on hard work and faith. Not on the legacy of a man who's been missing for decades. If you want answers about Dalton, I suggest you look somewhere else."

"What about Peter Collins?" Beth asked pointedly.

Joseph froze for a beat, then recovered. "What about him?"

"He works here, doesn't he? As your youth minister?"

Joseph's lips pressed into a thin line. "Peter Collins is a valued member of our team. Whatever speculation you've heard about him is irrelevant to the work he does here."

Thomas leaned forward. "And Heidi Collins? There are rumors she approached you years ago, claiming Peter was your son."

Joseph's voice dropped, quiet but laced with steel. "Heidi Collins has nothing at all to do with Edward Dalton. Rumors are just that... rumors. Heidi Collins made baseless accusations, and they were proven false. There's nothing more to say."

Beth met his gaze. "And the paternity test? It ruled you out as Peter's father?"

Joseph's eyes hardened. "Yes. And that's the end of it."

Thomas lifted a brow. "So, you deny any connection to Peter or Heidi Collins?"

"Absolutely," Joseph said, his voice clipped. "And I won't entertain this line of questioning any further. These are baseless claims from decades ago."

"That's funny," Thomas quipped. "We were told that Peter Collins has been proven to be a descendent of Edward Dalton. His DNA was tested against Sheriff Piper's, Matthew Thompson's, and Emily Johnson's."

Joseph stood. "I won't listen to any more of your accusations."

Beth closed her notebook slowly, rising to her feet. "Thank you for your time, Pastor Wright. We'll let you get back to your work."

Joseph's gaze followed her, sharp and unyielding. "I hope you do. Because this conversation is over."

The heat outside felt heavier as Beth and Thomas stepped into the late afternoon sun, the sleek exterior of Wright Way Church towering behind them. The earlier buzz of activity in the atrium had felt almost oppressive. An unsettling silence replaced it.

Thomas ran a hand through his hair, glancing over his shoulder. "He was lying. About all of it."

Beth didn't look back. Her steps were deliberate as they crossed the parking lot. "That much was obvious."

They reached the car, and Beth leaned against the hood, flipping open her notebook. "But the real question is, what was he lying about? And why?"

Thomas rubbed the bridge of his nose. "The way he dodged anything about Edward Dalton, Heidi, and Peter Collins. It wasn't just denial. It was defensive. He knows something, even if he refuses to admit it."

Beth scribbled a few quick notes before tapping her pen against the edge of her notebook. "And his refusal to acknowledge any connection to Edward Dalton felt rehearsed, like he's had years to perfect that response."

Thomas nodded, then frowned. "And yet...did you notice how he didn't outright deny that Edward influenced the early days of this church? He just said it had nothing to do with him."

"Deflection," Beth said. "The same with Peter. The paternity test may have ruled him out officially, but we don't know what strings were pulled to make that happen."

Thomas glanced at her, his jaw tightening. "You're thinking Martin Wright covered for him?"

Beth sighed. "It's a possibility. Reverend Martin Wright was just as guarded. If anyone would protect Joseph's reputation, it would be him."

Thomas leaned against the car beside her, folding his arms. "So what's next? We've hit a wall with Joseph."

Beth continued to tap her pen against her notebook thoughtfully. "Next, we dig into the details he doesn't want us to find. There are records somewhere. Church financials, property deeds, revival schedules from Dalton's era. Something that ties these pieces together."

"And Heidi Collins?" Thomas asked. "Do we try to find her?"

Beth paused, considering. "If she's willing to talk, she could fill in some blanks. But I wouldn't count on Joseph or Martin Wright making it easy for us to track her down."

Thomas frowned. "Do you think she's still in Dallas?"

Beth closed her notebook, her expression resolute. "If she's not, I'm sure Samuel Piper knows where she is. People like Joseph Wright don't let their loose ends wander far. I just don't know how much she can give us on Edward Dalton. Her connection is with Joseph Wright."

They climbed into the car, the tension from the meeting still lingering. As they pulled out of the parking lot, Beth glanced at the imposing church in the rearview mirror.

"Joseph might believe this conversation is over," she breathed. "But he's wrong."

13

Constantine stepped out of room eight at the Puckerbrush Motel, a small, wrapped gift tucked under her arm. The crisp spring air carried the earthy scent of fresh rain, mingling with the faint sweetness of blooming wildflowers from the nearby fields. A soft breeze ruffled her hair as she crossed the gravel lot, her shoes crunching against the damp stones. She felt lighter than she had in days, looking forward to the warmth of dinner with Abigail and Matthew. It was her first chance to see Archer and Grace since arriving in Puckerbrush.

As she reached the edge of the lot, the rumble of an approaching car drew her attention. A dark sedan pulled into a nearby spot, its headlights cutting through the soft glow of twilight. She paused instinctively, watching as two figures emerged from the vehicle.

The man stepped out first, tall and broad-shouldered, stretching as he exited the car. His dark hair was slightly tousled, and he exuded a quiet confidence. A moment later, a woman followed, her sharp features framed by a purposeful expression as she adjusted the strap of a well-worn leather satchel.

It was Dr. Harper and Thomas Everett. She hadn't spoken to them earlier in the café, but now, their presence felt more immediate, as though fate had conspired to bring their paths together.

Thomas glanced toward her, his eyes locking on hers with a flicker of surprise that quickly softened into curiosity. It was as if the rest of the world fell away, leaving only the hum of the breeze and the distant song of birds. He offered a small, hesitant smile.

"Evening," he said, his voice smooth and low, carrying just enough warmth to hint at the person beneath the traveler's weariness.

"Good evening," Constantine replied, clutching the gift a little tighter as she returned the smile.

Dr. Harper stepped forward. Her tone was polite but edged with the curiosity of someone accustomed to asking questions. "You're Constantine Thornton, aren't you? Emily at the café mentioned your name."

"I am," Constantine said.

"Dr. Elizabeth Harper," the woman introduced herself with a nod. "And this is Thomas Everett. I'm a historian, and we're here researching Edward Dalton. I've read your book on the history of Puckerbrush. It's fascinating."

Constantine felt Thomas's gaze linger on her, steady and thoughtful. "Puckerbrush has a lot of stories," she said, though the mention of Edward Dalton stirred a faint unease. "But I wouldn't call myself a historian."

"Even so," Thomas said, stepping closer, his tone earnest. "I imagine you've uncovered things that most people wouldn't notice. You seem like someone who's good at finding meaning in detail."

Constantine lifted an eyebrow, surprised by the unexpected compliment. "Well, I can't say I know what you're looking for, but I'm sure Puckerbrush will give you plenty to think about."

"That's the hope," Thomas replied, his smile softening. "And maybe if we're lucky, we'll run into someone who can help us find what we're looking for."

There was something in his voice, unassuming yet magnetic, that made Constantine want to stay, to ask more questions. But the gift in her hand reminded her of her destination, and she forced herself to take a step back.

"I'd love to chat more," she said, her voice softening, "but I'm late for dinner. Maybe another time."

Thomas hesitated, his eyes searching hers as if he wanted to say something more. Then he nodded. "Another time, then. Enjoy your evening."

"You too," Constantine said, turning toward the street.

As she walked away, she couldn't help but glance back. Thomas was still watching her, a faint smile on his face, before he turned to Dr. Harper with a quiet laugh. Constantine shook her head and smiled to herself, a strange warmth blooming inside her. There was something about him. A steadiness she hadn't realized she'd been missing.

Maybe, she thought as she headed toward Abigail and Matthew's house, spring was the season of new beginnings.

14

Constantine stepped onto the front porch of Abigail and Matthew's house, the faint glow of dusk settling over Puckerbrush. The familiar creak of the wooden floorboards under her feet brought a bittersweet smile as she balanced the gift and knocked lightly.

The door opened almost immediately. Abigail stood there, her smile warm and welcoming. "Come on in," she said, stepping aside. "We've been waiting for you."

The soft, cooing sound of baby Grace floated from the living room, where Matthew cradled her in his arms. Five-year-old Archer darted past them, giggling as he pushed a toy car along the floor.

Constantine crouched down to Archer's level. "Hey, big guy. How's my favorite troublemaker?"

Archer grinned, holding up his car proudly. "I'm not a trouble-maker today! Daddy said I'm a helper!"

Matthew chuckled from the armchair. "Helper with conditions."

Constantine handed Archer the small gift. "Well, this is for my favorite helper." She winked, watching his eyes light up as he tore into the wrapping to reveal a set of small, colorful books.

"Books!" he squealed, running to show Abigail, who gave Constantine a grateful smile.

Matthew shifted Grace slightly in his arms and stood. "She's been fussy all afternoon. I'm hoping you're the baby whisperer tonight." He passed the bundle to Constantine, who took her gently.

Grace blinked up at Constantine, her tiny hands curling and uncurling against her sweater. "Hi, sweet girl," Constantine murmured. The baby gurgled in response, and Constantine couldn't help but feel a wave of warmth. She walked with Grace toward the kitchen, where Abigail was finishing dinner. "Can I help you with anything?"

"You're helping already. Grace seems happy to see you." Abigail smiled. "Dinner is ready. If you want to take a seat."

The table was set simply, with bowls of hearty stew, fresh rolls, and a pitcher of iced tea. Abigail passed Archer his plate while Matthew sat at the head of the table, a soft smile lingering as he watched Grace nestle contentedly in Constantine's arms.

"So," Matthew began, his tone conversational, "what's new at the motel? Quiet, as always?"

Constantine smiled faintly, shifting Grace slightly. "Not exactly. I ran into Dr. Harper and Thomas Everett as I was leaving earlier."

Matthew and Abigail exchanged a brief glance, subtle but enough for Constantine to notice. She didn't mention it, but the weight of their unspoken exchange settled in the air between them.

"Harper and Everett," Matthew repeated, leaning back in his chair. "What did they want?"

"Not much," Constantine replied, brushing a hand lightly over Grace's soft hair. "Dr. Harper introduced herself as a historian researching Edward Dalton. Thomas said little, but he seemed... curious."

"They've been making the rounds," Abigail said, handing Archer a second roll. "They stopped by the museum the same day you did. They asked about Dalton, looked at some of the old flyers and clippings."

Matthew nodded. His tone was casual. "Same with me. I had a

chat with them at the café just as I was heading to the office. Harper's thorough. I'll give her that."

"What'd you tell them?" Constantine asked, trying to sound just as unconcerned, though her curiosity burned brighter now.

"Enough to satisfy them," Abigail said. "The museum's public records have nothing about Dalton that isn't already common knowledge." She paused, meeting Constantine's gaze. "And that's how it'll stay."

"Exactly," Matthew added, his tone easy but firm. "They're not here to cause trouble. They just want to connect the dots. If we're careful about what we share, there's no harm done. I got a call from Piper. He said they visited him."

"Piper?" Constantine asked. "What did he tell them?"

"With Lydia being pregnant and his need to protect Penelope, he sent them to Martin and Joseph Wright," Matthew explained.

"That must be where they were returning from tonight when I ran into them in the motel parking lot. Thomas was stretching like he had been in the car awhile," Constantine said.

"I would have loved to have been a fly on the wall for that conversation." Matthew laughed.

Constantine nodded slowly. She wanted to believe there was nothing to worry about, but the mention of Edward Dalton always carried a weight. The family's secret about Eldon and the true events of Dalton's disappearance loomed large, even if they'd learned to keep it well hidden.

"Did they say how long they'd be in town?" she asked, settling Grace against her shoulder as the baby let out a contented sigh.

"Not really," Abigail said, leaning back in her chair. "But I'd guess a few more days, maybe a week. Long enough to poke around and decide there's nothing left to find." Her smile softened. "It's not the first time someone's come here looking for answers about Edward Dalton, and it probably won't be the last. Puckerbrush doesn't give up its stories easily. Trust me, I know."

Matthew chuckled. "That's the truth. If they think they're the first ones to come asking about Dalton, they've got another thing coming.

Abigail holds the trophy for the first person to discover the truth about him."

Archer piped up between bites of stew, "Who's Dalton?"

"Just someone Aunt Constantine is helping people learn about, sweetheart," Abigail said, brushing a crumb off his cheek.

Constantine smiled at the boy's innocent curiosity but couldn't shake the unease from hearing Edward Dalton's name spoken so casually. She glanced at Abigail and Matthew, who both seemed perfectly at ease, but she knew better. Beneath their calm exteriors lay years of practice. Perfecting the art of keeping secrets buried.

Later, after the table was cleared, and the children put to bed, Constantine joined Abigail on the back porch. The night was cool and quiet, the faint scent of lilacs drifting on the breeze.

"Abigail," Constantine began hesitantly, her voice low. "Are you really not worried about Dr. Harper and Thomas Everett?"

Abigail didn't answer immediately. She leaned against the railing, her gaze distant. "It's not them I'm worried about," she said. "It's what happens if they dig too deep, like I did."

Constantine nodded. The unspoken truth was heavy between them. "You think they'll find out the truth like you did?"

"I think they'll leave with more questions than answers. I had Eldon to answer my questions," Abigail said with quiet confidence. She turned to Constantine, her voice softening. "But it's important we stay ahead of this. We can't let curiosity stir up old shadows. For Eldon's sake. You, me, and Matthew are the only people who know the truth about what happened to Edward Dalton. We should keep it that way."

Constantine met Abigail's steady gaze, the weight of their shared burden settling once more. "I understand."

"Good," Abigail said, her expression softening into a small smile. "And don't let them distract you too much, especially Thomas. He's got a kind face. But remember why he's here."

Constantine chuckled softly, but the sound was tinged with nervousness. "I'll keep that in mind."

15

The warm aroma of freshly brewed coffee and the low hum of conversation greeted Constantine. The Puckerbrush Café was alive with its usual morning energy. Local patrons chatted over steaming plates, and the clink of cutlery created a rhythmic backdrop.

Constantine paused near the entrance, scanning the room. Her eyes landed on a corner table, and her breath hitched.

Thomas Everett sat alone, a mug of coffee beside him and a notebook open in front of him. His dark hair was slightly disheveled, and he looked up just as she hesitated. Their eyes met, and his warm, easy smile sent an unexpected flicker of heat through her.

"Good morning, Constantine," he called, his tone friendly.

She considered turning around, making an excuse about needing to grab a coffee to go. But Emily's voice cut through her thoughts.

"Morning, Constantine," Emily said as she walked past, a coffeepot in hand. "You want your usual spot?"

Thomas gestured to the empty seat across from him. "Or you could join me," he offered. "Breakfast is always better with company."

She hesitated, glancing at Emily, who paused nearby with a

curious look. "Sure," Constantine said, forcing herself to smile as she crossed the room.

As she slid into the seat across from Thomas, Emily stepped forward with her coffeepot. "What can I get you, Constantine? The usual?"

Constantine nodded. "Thanks, Emily. And maybe an extra coffee. I have a feeling it's one of those mornings."

Emily smiled knowingly, pouring her a cup. "You got it. Let me know if you need anything else." Her gaze lingered briefly on Thomas before she headed back toward the kitchen.

Thomas waited until Emily was out of earshot before leaning forward slightly, resting his elbows on the table. "She's great. Friendly, too. You all know each other well, huh?"

"Everyone knows everyone in Puckerbrush," Constantine said, picking up her coffee. "I learned that after I accidentally arrived here."

Thomas tilted his head, intrigued. "Accidentally? I assumed you were visiting like Dr. Harper and me since I saw you at the Pucker-brush Motel."

She nodded, her smile faint but genuine. "I was driving to Millerton to see what I could find out about my great-grandmother's brother, and my car began acting up. I took the next exit off the inter-state, which happened to be Puckerbrush." She watched his expres-sion closely, her tone growing softer. "While I was here, I learned the great-great-uncle I was looking for had lived here most of his life. It was like fate was guiding me."

Thomas's eyebrows lifted. His interest was clearly piqued. "And you didn't know he was here?"

"Not at all," Constantine replied. "It's a crazy coincidence. You know the show *Tracing Your Heritage*?"

"I do," Thomas said, nodding. "That's what brought us here."

"They were here taping the segment with Matthew Thompson, Emily Johnson, and Samuel Piper. I watched the taping out of curiosity and overheard Matthew mention someone named Eldon. Afterward, I asked him about it, and one thing led to another." She paused, her smile widening. "That's how I found out Eldon was the great-great-uncle I was looking for."

Thomas leaned back slightly. His expression was thoughtful. "That's...incredible. Like you said, it really sounds like fate."

"It felt like it," Constantine admitted, stirring her coffee idly. "I'd been chasing this story for years, and then to stumble into the one place where it all connected..." she trailed off, her voice tinged with wonder and just a hint of something else. Something guarded.

Thomas's gaze lingered on her, his curiosity evident. "So, you stayed? Decided to dig in and see what you could uncover?"

"Something like that," Constantine replied, carefully deflecting. "Puckerbrush has a way of pulling people in."

"Tell me about it," Thomas said with a soft chuckle. "I came here looking for answers about Edward Dalton, and now I feel like every corner of this town has another piece of the story. It's...overwhelming sometimes, but exciting, too."

Constantine nodded, though the mention of Dalton sent a ripple of unease through her. "That's Puckerbrush for you. Always full of surprises.

"It's slow going," he admitted, stirring sugar into his coffee. "The more I dig, the harder it is to figure out who Dalton really was. My family made him out to be a hero, but the things I've uncovered..." He shook his head. "They don't fit that story."

Constantine's chest tightened. "What doesn't fit?"

Thomas's gaze grew thoughtful. "The letters and records we've found. There's evidence of missing funds, people who felt misled after his revivals, and the relatives I have that I or my family never knew about. Piper, Emily, and Matthew. It's tough to square with the image I grew up with. I want to believe he was a good man, but it feels...complicated."

Constantine focused on her coffee, stirring it slowly to steady her nerves. "Legends have a way of growing over time," she said. "People remember what they want to remember, not always what's true."

Thomas nodded, a small frown tugging at his lips. "That's exactly what Dr. Harper says. She's determined to uncover the truth, no matter what it is. I just hope..." He trailed off, then shook his head. "Never mind."

"What?" Constantine prompted, despite herself.

He hesitated, then met her gaze. "I just hope it's not worse than I'm ready to handle. It's my family, you know? It's hard to question the stories you grew up with."

His honesty disarmed her, and for a fleeting moment, Constantine wanted to tell him the truth. To let him see the real Edward Dalton, the man behind the myth. But then she thought of Abigail and Matthew and the years their family had worked to keep that truth buried.

"You might not like what you find," she breathed, her voice steady but distant. "Sometimes the truth isn't worth the cost."

Thomas studied her, his expression unreadable. "Do you believe that? That it's better to leave some things buried?"

Her heart raced, but she forced a small smile. "I think it depends on what's at stake."

Their conversation paused as Emily returned with Constantine's breakfast. "Here you go," Emily said, her smile bright but tinged with curiosity. She glanced between Constantine and Thomas. "Enjoy your meal."

"Thanks, Emily," Constantine said, relieved for the brief reprieve.

By the time they finished breakfast, the tension had eased slightly. Thomas leaned back in his chair. His expression was relaxed.

"Thanks for joining me," he said. "I wasn't expecting company, but I'm glad you came."

Constantine smiled faintly. "Me too. It was nice."

As she stood to leave, Emily appeared again, clearing their plates. "You two have a good day," she said, her tone cheerful but still curious.

"You too," Thomas said, offering her a polite smile.

The crisp spring air greeted Constantine as she stepped outside the café, the soft hum of Main Street filling the quiet space around her. She glanced down the road, where sunlight dappled the cobblestones and wildflowers peeked through cracks along the sidewalk.

Behind her, the café door jingled again, and she turned to see Thomas stepping out, his notebook tucked under one arm. He paused when he saw her, a faint smile forming on his lips.

"Heading somewhere interesting?" he asked, his tone light.

The instinct to deflect gnawed at her core. But something about his presence, his amiable smile, and his calm curiosity made her pause. She glanced down the street again, the quiet charm of Puckerbrush pulling at her.

"Not really," she said. "But if you're not in a hurry, I could show you around."

Thomas blinked, surprised, before his smile widened. "You'd do that?"

"Sure," Constantine replied, her voice casual. "Puckerbrush isn't big, but it has its moments."

"I'd like that," he said, his tone warm.

As they strolled through Puckerbrush's streets, Thomas turned to Constantine, curiosity flickering in his expression.

"You mentioned Millerton earlier," he said. "It sounded familiar. I read through my notebook, and it was one town listed on my great-grandfather's revival tours. Did you ever make it there?"

Constantine nodded, her lips curving into a faint smile. "I did. Abigail and I drove there not long after I arrived in Puckerbrush. It was...overwhelming, to say the least."

"What did you find?" Thomas asked, his tone both gentle and intrigued.

She hesitated, glancing at the cobblestones beneath her feet before speaking. "We found the old homestead where my great-grandmother and her brother, Eldon, grew up. It was tucked away in a field, nearly swallowed by wildflowers and time, but it was still standing."

His steps slowed as he looked at her, his brow furrowing. "That must've been incredible to see."

"It was," Constantine said. "We found records at the county clerk's office and even some old articles in the library. Their family lost the house during the Great Depression. Abigail and I could almost feel the weight of that loss when we stood there."

"What happened to them?" Thomas asked, his voice laced with concern.

Constantine took a steadying breath. "Their parents couldn't take care of them anymore. They traded my great-grandmother to a farmer in exchange for a truck. Eldon...he was abandoned on a dirt road not far from here." Her voice wavered, but she kept her gaze steady.

Thomas's expression darkened. "That's horrible."

"It is," she agreed. "But it also explains so much about the stories my great-grandmother used to tell me. Stories of resilience and longing. She never stopped wondering what happened to Eldon. Finding even pieces of the truth felt like I was bringing some closure to my family."

Thomas was quiet a second before speaking, "It sounds like you've been on quite a journey. To piece all of that together. It's no small thing."

Constantine shrugged lightly, though her voice carried an undercurrent of pride. "I've had help. Puckerbrush has a way of connecting people to their past. To each other."

He smiled faintly. "I'm seeing that. And I think you're right. Sometimes, it's not just about finding answers. It's about the connections you make along the way. I hope I can make some connections that can help me find out what happened to my great-grandfather."

Constantine's step faltered, but she recovered quickly, her expression carefully neutral. "I'm sure you will," she said, her tone steady but distant.

As they walked, the gentle hum of the town rose around them, filling the quiet spaces left by their words. Sharing her story had eased one burden, but in its place, a new unease crept in. An ache born of unspoken truths. Their stories mirrored each other in unexpected ways. They were both searching for answers to piece together the fractured legacies of their families. She had found her truth, but she also carried the key to his. And like so many secrets in Pucker-brush, it was not one easily surrendered.

16

The park was quiet at this time of day, sunlight dappling the cobblestones and the soft murmur of spring filling the air. Constantine led Thomas to a weathered bench near a small fountain, its gentle trickle adding to the tranquil atmosphere.

"This is one of my favorite spots in town," she said as she sat down, gesturing to the open green expanse framed by budding trees.

Thomas settled beside her, his notebook resting on his lap. "It's beautiful. Feels like the kind of place where you can catch your breath."

Constantine nodded, her gaze drifting to the fountain. "That's exactly why I like it."

They sat in silence before Constantine glanced at him. "So, what's it like working with Dr. Harper? She seems...intense."

Thomas chuckled. "She is. Brilliant and demanding, but she pushes me to be better. Edward Dalton's story means a lot to me, and it's become important to her, too."

"What makes it so important?" Constantine asked.

Thomas hesitated. His gaze was distant. "Dalton was a giant in my family's history. Growing up, we heard stories about his revivals, his impact on people's lives. But the more I dig, the more I realize how much we don't know. Not just about who he was, but about what happened to him."

"What do you mean?" Constantine leaned forward slightly.

"He disappeared in 1961," Thomas said, his brow furrowing. "After one of his revivals, he just...vanished. No letters, no records, no explanations. It's like the world swallowed him up."

"That's a big mystery to solve." She paused for a beat before asking, "What happens if you figure it out?"

Thomas turned to her, his expression thoughtful. "I'm not sure. I want to preserve his story, but I also want it to be the actual story. Not just the one my family passed down. The truth, whatever it turns out to be."

Constantine nodded, her fingers brushing the edge of the bench, realizing she could give him part of the answer to what he was searching for. "That's a lot to take on."

"It is," he admitted. "But it feels worth it. If there's one thing I've learned, it's that history deserves honesty."

Before she could respond, he leaned back, his tone lightening. "What about you, though?"

She arched a brow. "What about me?"

"You've told me about your family history," Thomas said with a slight smile. "But what about you? Do you have a boyfriend or husband back home? Where is home?"

The question caught her off guard, and she hesitated.

"No," she said, her voice steady but tinged with something quieter. "No boyfriend. Not anymore."

Thomas blinked, his expression softening. "Not anymore?"

Constantine traced a pattern on the bench with her finger, her gaze distant. "We broke up a few months ago. He traveled a lot for work, and we barely saw each other. I teach creative writing at a community college in the city. It was hard for me to travel with him. Eventually, it felt like we were living separate lives. We just...grew apart."

"That sounds hard," Thomas said.

"It was," Constantine admitted, glancing at him briefly. "But it was the right decision. Afterward, I needed to clear my head. Spend time with people who actually know me. That's part of why I came back here."

"To Puckerbrush?"

She nodded. "It felt like the right place to be. It's quiet, familiar. Abigail and Matthew are here. This town has a way of grounding you, whether you want it to or not."

Thomas smiled faintly. "Sounds like it's been good for you."

"It has," Constantine said, her voice soft. Then she tilted her head slightly, her curiosity sparking. "What about you?"

He blinked. "What about me?"

"Where's home? What is your occupation? Are you seeing anyone?" she asked, her tone light but her gaze steady.

He hesitated, scratching the back of his neck. "No. I'm not seeing anyone. Not right now."

"By choice?" she asked, echoing his earlier phrasing.

Thomas laughed softly, shaking his head. "Touché. I guess you could say it's by circumstance. I also teach. History in Fairview. That's how I met Dr. Harper. Between work and all the traveling I've been doing for this project, there's little room left for anything else."

Constantine nodded knowingly. "I can understand that."

He looked at her, his smile turning slightly apologetic. "And honestly, I haven't been looking. Too much on my plate as it is."

"Fair enough," she said, her lips curving into a faint smile. He trusted her. She could see it in his steady gaze. But trust could be dangerous. If she let him in, if she told him what really happened, would he still look at her that way?

They fell into a comfortable silence, the soft sounds of the fountain filling the gaps. After a moment, Thomas shifted slightly and turned toward her. "I don't know about you, but this trip to Pucker-brush feels like a bit of a gift. We should make the most of it."

Constantine tilted her head with a questioning look. "What do you mean?"

"Well," Thomas said, his tone light, "how about dinner tonight?

I'm here for a few more days. It would be nice to sit down and talk more without a fountain distracting me."

Constantine chuckled. "I think I could manage that. But if you're staying a while, I've got an idea."

"Oh?" he asked, looking intrigued.

"I could show you Millerton. If you're up for it. Maybe where my great-grandmother and great-great-uncle started out, and where your great-grandfather held a revival."

Thomas smiled, his interest clearly piqued. "That sounds perfect. Dinner tonight and a tour of Millerton. It's a deal."

Constantine extended a hand playfully. "Deal."

He took her hand, holding it longer than expected. "I'm looking forward to it."

The conversation turned lighter as they mapped out their plans, the tension of the past giving way to the promise of something new. As the sunlight dipped lower, painting the park in golden hues, an unexpected spark of excitement went through her. A sense that her guardedness was giving way to possibility.

17

It was early evening as they drove through quiet fields on the way to Millerton. Constantine sat in the passenger seat, her hands resting on a notebook in her lap.

"You know," she began, breaking the companionable silence, "My great-grandmother only ever said Millerton was the place where her first memories began. No stories, no details...just that."

Thomas glanced at her, clearly intrigued. "That's all? Nothing about what she did there?"

She shook her head. "Nothing. Just the story of her parents trading her to a farmer for his truck and then driving off with her brother, Eldon, in the back." Constantine paused. "I think she probably wanted to forget the rest."

"I don't blame her," Thomas said. "It sounds like today is going to be as much a discovery for you as it is for me."

"Exactly," she said, her tone quiet. "If you take a left at the next stop sign, I can show you the house where my great-grandmother lived."

Thomas followed her directions and continued down the gravel road, passing a farmhouse now and then.

"We're almost there." Constantine pointed ahead. "I hope I'm remembering my directions correctly. It's been a while since Abigail and I visited."

"I'll slow down so we don't miss it," Thomas said.

"I believe it's the next house." Constantine pointed toward the right side of the road. "Yes, there it is. That's it. You can turn in here."

Thomas slowed down, taking in the view of a dilapidated farmhouse. Broken windows and the screen door hanging from its hinges. "Right here?" he asked.

As he placed the car in park, Constantine had already opened her door. Thomas joined her on the weed-covered gravel drive.

"This is where your great-grandmother lived?" he asked, studying the rundown building. "It's amazing to think a place like this held so many memories and so much loss."

"Until she was ten years old. Eldon was five." Constantine began walking toward the porch.

"Are you sure it's safe?" Thomas asked. "Maybe we shouldn't go in."

"You might be right." She shivered. The structure was old and rickety. Even more than when she and Abigail were here before. She was more concerned about the sense of melancholy and loss that hovered low.

"I'm getting hungry," he said. "We should find someplace to have dinner."

"We should." Gratitude coursed through her at his perceptiveness. "I remember seeing a café on Main Street when Abigail and I came here. They should still be open."

"There's nothing better than a burger from a small-town café." Thomas chuckled.

They climbed back into the car and drove back down the gravel road. As they crested a hill, Millerton came into view, a small cluster of historic buildings nestled among rolling hills. Its tidy streets and old-fashioned charm made it seem almost frozen in time.

He slowed the car, taking in the scene. "It's smaller than I imagined, but there's something peaceful about it."

Constantine nodded. "I remember thinking the same thing when

I first came here. It feels like a place where the past lingers, just waiting to be uncovered."

They parked near the town square, where a modest fountain bubbled softly at the center of a cobblestone plaza. Constantine stepped out of the car, spotting the plaque she and Abigail discovered, which named her family as one of the founding families of Millerton. She ran her fingers over the plaque, the engraved names stirring a mix of pride and sadness. "It's strange to think they were part of this town's foundation, but their story feels so incomplete."

"Where do we start?" Thomas asked, joining her.

She gestured vaguely toward the main road. "There's no real plan. Last time, Abigail and I just wandered around, trying to soak it in. Let's see what we find."

The two of them strolled through the streets, their footsteps echoing softly in the stillness. The buildings were small and weathered, their facades bearing the marks of time.

"This feels like stepping into a story," Thomas remarked, his voice low.

"It does," Constantine agreed. "But without the plot. Just the setting, waiting for someone to fill it in."

A narrow side street caught Constantine's eye as they reached the edge of town. At its end stood a small, unassuming restaurant with a wooden sign that read *Millie's Table*.

Constantine tilted her head. "There it is."

Thomas glanced at the cozy-looking building, its warm lights spilling onto the street. "What do you think?"

She smiled. "Why not? I'm curious."

The restaurant was inviting, its mismatched furniture and glowing lanterns giving it a rustic charm. The smell of baked bread and simmering herbs greeted them as they stepped inside.

The hostess seated them by a window, and Constantine glanced over the menu. "This feels like the perfect find for a day like this. Completely unplanned, but just right."

Thomas grinned. "Sometimes the best discoveries are the ones you stumble on."

Their conversation flowed easily as they ordered and waited for their meals. Constantine spoke about the fragments of her great-grandmother's life she'd pieced together, and Thomas shared the challenges of reconstructing Edward Dalton's story.

When their food arrived, the plates were filled with simple, comforting dishes that seemed to reflect the town itself.

"This might be the best surprise of the day," she said after her first bite of the mystery casserole.

Thomas raised his glass of soda with a smile. "Here's to surprises and to filling in the blanks."

Constantine clinked her glass against his, a warm laugh escaping her lips.

After dinner, they wandered the quiet streets of Millerton, the lamplight casting long shadows on the cobblestones.

"It's strange," she said, her gaze wandering to the darkened windows of a nearby shop. "I feel like I'm looking at something I should recognize, but I don't. It's like trying to remember a dream."

Thomas nodded, walking beside her. "Maybe that's why you're here. To make sense of it."

As they returned to the car, the weight of the past seemed to blend with the quiet promise of the present.

The rain started softly as they left Millerton, gentle droplets tapping against the windshield as Thomas steered the car back toward Puckerbrush.

The evening had been...nice. Easy, steady. Dinner was filled with warm conversation and laughter, and there were moments when Constantine caught herself watching the way Thomas's eyes softened when he smiled. She hadn't expected that. She hadn't expected to feel so at ease.

But now, as the rain thickened into heavy sheets, the quiet hum of the wipers filled the space between them.

Thomas slowed the car, squinting through the downpour. "This is turning into a mess. I think we'll have to pull over for a bit."

Constantine nodded, hugging her arms loosely across her chest as he eased the car onto a narrow side road beneath a cluster of trees.

The rain was relentless now, drumming on the roof with a steady pulse that seemed to seal them in together, the world beyond the fogged windows dissolving into shadows.

For a long moment, neither spoke.

Thomas finally broke the silence, leaning back slightly in his seat. "Well, at least we're not on the highway. I've had worse dates."

Constantine lifted one brown in silent question, lips curving despite herself. "Dates, huh? So this was a date now?"

His mouth opened and then closed. He gave a sheepish shrug. "I mean...dinner...a scenic drive. Sudden weather event. If it's not a date, it's feeling suspiciously like one."

She laughed, shaking her head as she stared out the rain-streaked window. "So, this is your idea of romance? Stranding me in a thunderstorm?"

He tilted his head thoughtfully. "Could be worse. I could've brought you to one of those chain restaurants with sticky menus and terrible coffee."

"Oh, Millerton's finest diner with the mystery casserole was an upgrade?" she teased, warmth spreading through her chest.

Thomas grinned, leaning his elbow on the center console. "Hey, the pie was solid. And for the record, I'm not the one who ordered the casserole."

She rolled her eyes, but the smile lingered. "You're never going to let me live that down, are you?"

"Not a chance." His voice softened, his gaze lingering just a little longer now. "But...for what it's worth, I had a great time tonight."

The rain softened slightly, tapering into a steady rhythm, and the air inside the car felt warmer.

Constantine shifted, glancing at him from the corner of her eye. "Me too."

For a heartbeat, the quiet between them wasn't awkward. It was charged. They were both aware of something, but neither had quite figured out how to name it yet.

Thomas cleared his throat, voice gentler now. "So...since we're stuck here, tell me something. Something you rarely share with people."

Constantine blinked, caught off guard. "What, like a confession?"

"Sure. Or something random. Anything." He smiled, playful again. "I'll even go first if you need inspiration."

She smirked. "Go for it."

He leaned back, considering for a moment. "Alright. I once entered a pie-eating contest at a county fair. Lost spectacularly. There's a photo somewhere of me, completely covered in cherry filling, looking like I regretted every life choice leading to that moment."

Constantine snorted, covering her mouth. "I need to see this picture immediately."

"Absolutely not. That evidence is sealed for the safety of everyone involved."

She grinned, but his expression softened, waiting.

Constantine hesitated, feeling the vulnerability creeping in but wanting to meet his openness halfway. She tucked a strand of hair behind her ear.

"Okay, um...I used to play the piano. Badly. Like, so badly, my music teacher suggested I try a 'less stressful' hobby." She made air quotes with her fingers.

Thomas raised an eyebrow. "Less stressful than music? What'd you switch to?"

"Writing. But I wasn't much better at first. Lots of angsty poetry. You know, the tragic, world-ending, heartbreak kind."

He grinned. "So you were a poet and didn't know it?"

She groaned. "You did not just say that."

"I absolutely did."

The laughter came easier now, filling the car with something lighter than the storm outside.

And then, just as the rain slowed even further, Thomas grew quiet again, his gaze softening as he looked at her.

"Constantine."

Her heart fluttered unexpectedly at the way he said her name. Like he was trying to memorize it.

"Yeah?"

He exhaled, the teasing smile fading. "I like this. Being around you. I know we've both been guarded, but tonight felt different. And I'd like to keep getting to know you, if you'll let me."

The vulnerability in his voice caught her off guard. She felt the truth of it, the sincerity that made it impossible to deflect with another joke.

Her fingers curled into the hem of her sweater.

"I'd like that too," she whispered.

Outside, the rain slowed to a gentle drizzle, leaving behind a quiet she wasn't sure she wanted to break.

And for the first time in a long while, Constantine felt something other than the weight of the past. She felt a possibility.

18

The glow of the car's headlights cut through the night after the rainstorm. Outside, the fields and hills they'd passed earlier were cloaked in shadows. Their shapes softened by the deepening twilight. The hum of the tires against the asphalt was the only sound for a while, a quiet contrast to the thoughts swirling in Constantine's mind.

She leaned her head against the window, watching the blurred shapes of trees slipping past. The day had been heavier than she'd expected. It was filled with quiet revelations, fragments of history both shared and unspoken. And yet, it wasn't just the stories that lingered. It was the sense of connection she hadn't anticipated. The quiet way Thomas had listened, the way he hadn't pressed but had still understood. The way she wanted to tell him the truth.

The thought pressed deeply on her chest, the secret of Edward Dalton's fate clawing at the edges of her conscience. But even as it lingered, she stayed silent, because saying it aloud would mean betraying her family. The people who were her safe place.

A breath broke the quiet, followed by Thomas's voice, low and thoughtful. "Thanks for today," he said, his gaze fixed on the road.

"Going to Millerton, hearing about your great-grandmother... It was meaningful. I can see why it's such a big part of your life."

Constantine turned toward him, a smile playing on her lips. "Thank you for coming along. For listening."

Thomas glanced at her briefly, his features softened in the dim dashboard light. "I think it's important. Stories like hers deserve to be heard. And I'm glad you felt like you could tell me."

She hesitated, heart tightening, the words of confession rising to the back of her throat. *You don't know the whole story, Thomas. If you did, would you still trust me?* But she swallowed it back, pushing the thought away as she nodded.

"I did," she said, her voice tinged with genuine emotion. "And I appreciate that more than I can say. It's not just that you listened...it's that you understood. What it means to carry a story like this. I felt responsible to tell it right."

Thomas nodded, his hands steady on the wheel, the faint creases at the corners of his eyes deepening. "I understand. And sharing my story with you today...it felt different. Like it wasn't just about Edward Dalton, but about how his story connects to everything else." He paused, glancing her way again. "How it's shaped my family. How it's shaped me."

Constantine tilted her head, studying him in the soft glow of the dashboard. His honesty, the vulnerability just beneath his words, struck something deep inside her. How could she carry this secret, knowing how much it mattered to him?

"It's funny, isn't it?" she murmured, voice quieter now. "How sharing these pieces of ourselves makes them feel lighter."

"It does," Thomas agreed, his tone warm. "And it makes them more real, somehow."

The road curved gently, the first outlines of Puckerbrush emerging in the distance, the glow of streetlights casting soft halos through the mist settling in the fields. Thomas slowed the car as they approached the Puckerbrush Motel, pulling into the small lot where the neon sign buzzed faintly overhead. The stillness felt profound, the quiet that made it easier to hear the things left unsaid.

He shut off the engine, and neither moved. The sudden quiet settled around them, not awkward but charged as though the stillness itself was holding its breath.

Constantine finally spoke, her voice barely more than a whisper. "I just wanted to say... thank you. For today. For sharing your story with me. It means more than you know, Thomas."

He turned fully toward her then, his expression open and unguarded. "It means a lot to me, too. I don't share Dalton's story with just anyone. Not the deeper parts of it, anyway. But with you...it felt right."

The honesty in his voice was like a weight pressing against her ribs, and for a fleeting second, she felt the pull to tell him everything. But then came the fear. Of what it could unravel. Of how it could change the way he looked at her.

So, instead, she reached for the only truth she felt safe sharing.

"That means more than you know," she breathed, her voice steady despite the storm inside her.

Their eyes met, the silence between them deepening. Constantine could feel the magnetic pull, the quiet gravity drawing them together. Her heart raced, unsure yet certain all at once. And then, slowly, she leaned closer, her gaze dipping to his lips just as his hand brushed lightly against hers on the center console.

Thomas leaned in halfway. Their lips met softly, a kiss that was tentative but sure, the unspoken promise that words couldn't quite capture. It wasn't rushed. It wasn't dramatic. It was right. A quiet acknowledgment of everything they had shared, of the trust quietly forming between them.

And yet, as their lips parted, Constantine felt that ache return. The unspoken truth pressing heavily against her heart, threatening to fracture the moment.

She drew back just slightly, her cheeks flushed, but her smile remained. "Goodnight, Thomas."

He held her gaze for a lingering beat, his voice warm and steady. "Goodnight, Constantine."

She hesitated as she opened the car door and stepped out into the cool night air. Turning back, she caught one last glimpse of him still watching her, his expression thoughtful but content. She wanted to hold on to that look, the way he had seen her, not just the pieces she'd chosen to share.

But as she closed the door to her motel room behind her and leaned against it, her smile faded just a touch. Because even as the warmth lingered, so did the guilt.

You deserve the truth, Thomas. But I don't know how to give it to you without breaking everything I'm trying to protect.

For the first time in a long while, the night felt full of possibility, but it also felt like standing on the edge of a secret too heavy to keep.

19

The scent of lilacs drifted through the open window, mingling with the dampness of spring rain. Outside, the fields were quiet, washed in pale twilight; the calm felt almost too delicate.

The fire in Abigail's living room crackled softly, the orange glow warming the cozy space. Constantine sat curled on the edge of the armchair, fingers tracing invisible patterns against the fabric of her jeans. She wasn't sure how to start or how to explain the knot twisting tighter inside her since the day she and Thomas spent together.

Abigail sat across from her, watching quietly as she stirred the tea in her hands. She had that patient stillness about her, the kind that alluded she'd already noticed Constantine's restlessness and was just waiting for her to speak.

Finally, Constantine broke the silence. "I need your advice."

Abigail's eyebrows lifted slightly, but her smile was gentle. "Of course. What's on your mind?"

Constantine hesitated, staring into the flames as they licked the logs, searching for the right words. "It's about Thomas." She glanced up, her voice quieter now. "I think he trusts me. He's kind, Abigail. Genuine. But he's still searching for answers. About Edward Dalton.

And I…" She swallowed. "I don't know what to do. I could tell him the truth. I know it would help him. But I also know how much it could hurt this family."

Abigail set down her tea carefully, leaning forward with quiet understanding. "You care about him, don't you?"

Constantine nodded, voice barely above a whisper. "I do. But it's more than that. He deserves honesty. And yet, I don't know if I can give it to him. Not without breaking everything we've protected."

Abigail was silent, watching her closely. Then she spoke, her voice gentle but steady. "I know how hard this must feel. You're caught between wanting to help someone you care about and wanting to protect your family. And both things are good. But they're also complicated."

Constantine exhaled slowly, her fingers tightening around the hem of her sweater. "I feel like I'm lying to him by keeping this secret. He's not just curious, he's hurting. I can see it when he talks about his family. He's searching for answers because he feels like he's lost a piece of something. And I could give that to him." She paused. Her voice was thick with emotion. "But if I do, I risk everything. Eldon's memory. This town's trust. Our whole family."

Abigail nodded thoughtfully, her gaze never leaving Constantine's. "You're not lying, sweetheart. You're protecting a piece of history that was never yours to share in the first place." She paused, choosing her words carefully. "But what you do with that truth now? That must be your choice. I can't make it for you."

Constantine blinked, her chest tightening. "But you know what could happen if it comes out. If people find out what Eldon did."

"Yes." Abigail's voice softened even further. "And I won't pretend it wouldn't be hard. But Constantine, the truth isn't evil. It's just complicated. And sometimes, it stays buried for good reasons." She hesitated, then added, "But it doesn't mean you're wrong for wanting to share it. It means you must be sure you're sharing it for the right reasons."

Constantine frowned, shaking her head. "How do I know what the right reasons are? What if I make it worse?"

Abigail leaned forward, resting her hand gently over Constantine's. "You trust your heart. I know it feels impossible, but you have the kind of heart that won't let you act out of spite or selfishness. If you decide to tell Thomas, I trust you'll do it in a way that honors both the truth and our family."

Constantine swallowed. Her throat was tight. "And if I keep it to myself?"

Abigail squeezed her hand gently. "Then you're still protecting the people you love. That doesn't make you weak or dishonest. It makes you careful. And sometimes, being careful is the bravest thing you can do."

A log shifted in the fireplace, the scent of spring rain heavier now. Constantine let the quiet settle, trying to absorb Abigail's words. Trying to untangle the tight knot twisted in her chest.

Finally, she whispered, "I care about him, and I don't want to hurt him."

Abigail gave a sad smile. "I know. But you can't protect everyone from pain. Not forever. Sometimes, the truth has a way of finding its way out whether we're ready for it or not."

Constantine nodded slowly, the weight shifted inside her, though not quite easing. She wasn't sure what choice she would make yet. But at least now she understood it was hers to make.

And that, somehow, was both a comfort and a burden.

20

The scent of damp earth lingered in the early morning air as Constantine stepped out of her room at the Puckerbrush Motel. The pale sunlight had only just softened the mist clinging to the edges of town, making the cracked asphalt glisten underfoot. Birds stirred lazily from the pines beyond the lot, their songs a quiet contrast to the weight pressing on her chest.

She hadn't slept well. Not since spending the day with Thomas.

She'd enjoyed his company more than she expected. Too much, if she was being honest. It felt complicated. Familiar yet fragile. He was searching for answers about Edward Dalton, and Constantine knew all too well the cost of digging too deep into Puckerbrush's past. She had written that story already, or at least the version she could tell the world.

But there were still parts she'd left out. The parts that haunted her.

She adjusted the strap of her bag, intending to clear her head with a walk before heading to the café. But the sound of a door closing nearby caught her attention.

Elizabeth Harper stepped out of her room. The historian's sharp gaze locked onto Constantine instantly, and something in the way she held her satchel a little tighter made it clear that she wasn't out for a casual morning stroll.

Constantine drew in a steadying breath as Dr. Harper crossed the lot toward her, footsteps crisp against the damp gravel.

"Ms. Thornton," Dr. Harper greeted, her voice calm but far from casual. "I was hoping I might run into you."

Constantine forced a polite smile though her pulse quickened. "Morning, Dr. Harper. Early start?"

Her eyes narrowed slightly. "Habit. Research keeps me up at odd hours." She paused, studying Constantine. "I imagine you know how that feels. Your book was a very thorough work on your family's history here."

Constantine nodded, bracing herself. "Thanks. I tried to keep it honest."

Dr. Harper's expression didn't change. "I'm sure you did."

The words landed like a stone in Constantine's chest. She kept her voice steady. "I wrote about what I could verify. Anything else would have been speculation."

Dr. Harper took a step closer, her gaze unflinching. "Speculation is part of history, don't you think? Especially when the facts don't quite add up."

Constantine's grip tightened slightly on her bag. "If you're suggesting I left something out—"

"I'm suggesting there's more to the story than what made it into your book," Dr. Harper interrupted, her voice measured but firm. "You're close to Thomas. Spent the day together, didn't you? I'm sure you've had plenty of conversations about his great-grandfather."

Constantine's stomach knotted, but she kept her face neutral. "Thomas wants closure. That doesn't mean I have answers."

The historian's gaze sharpened, searching. "You and I both know Edward Dalton didn't just vanish, Ms. Thornton. People in this town remember things. They just choose silence when the truth gets uncomfortable."

The chill in the air suddenly felt sharper. Constantine swallowed, her heart pounding. She'd heard those same whispered truths when she first came to Puckerbrush. She'd seen the way the town protected its own, burying what couldn't be explained, or forgiven.

But she had kept her promise. She hadn't written everything. For Abigail. For Matthew. For Eldon's memory. And she wasn't about to break that now.

"I think you're reading too much into small-town gossip," Constantine said, voice calm but cold. "Puckerbrush has moved on. You should, too."

Dr. Harper's eyes narrowed. "My great-aunt Donna, didn't get the chance to 'move on.' She was nineteen when she attended one of Dalton's revivals. She gave him everything she had. Her faith, her savings. And when he left, she was broken. Not just spiritually. Financially. He preyed on people like her."

Constantine flinched, the words cutting deeper than expected. She knew of Dalton's charm. But hearing it now, so personal, made it harder to keep her guard up.

"I'm sorry for what happened to your great-aunt." She breathed. "But Edward Dalton is gone. And dredging this up after all these years won't bring closure. It'll just hurt people who had nothing to do with it."

Shaking her head, Dr. Harper whispered, "People don't just vanish. Not without help."

The words hung heavy between them, the damp morning air pressing against Constantine's chest. She knew what Dr. Harper was implying. And she couldn't let her keep pulling threads.

"I have nothing else to say," Constantine said, stepping back. "If you'll excuse me, I have somewhere to be."

The historian didn't stop her. But her parting words followed Constantine.

"I'll find the truth, Ms. Thornton. Whether or not you help me."

21

The sun filtered in through the large windows of the Puckerbrush Sheriff's Office, casting long, pale streaks across the scuffed wooden floor. Outside, the midday hush had settled over Main Street.

The front lobby was still. The steady tick of the wall clock echoed softly, joined only by the gentle rustle of papers beneath the slow churn of the desk fan. A half-full cup of coffee sat forgotten on the reception desk, its scent mingling with worn leather, wood polish, and the lingering trace of spring air drifting in from the open windows.

But behind the door marked *Sheriff Matthew Thompson*, the quiet felt heavier.

Constantine sat stiffly in a chair across from Matthew's desk, back straight, her shoulders tense, bracing for a conversation she wasn't sure how to start.

The sunlight caught the pale curve of Abigail's face, highlighting the worry in her eyes as she stood near the tall shelves of ledgers lining the wall, arms crossed. Her expression was unreadable but tight, her gaze pinned on Constantine with quiet concern.

Matthew leaned forward, elbows braced against the scarred wood of his desk, watching her closely. "What happened?" he asked, voice calm but edged with concern.

Constantine exhaled, releasing her grip on the bag strap. "It was Dr. Harper. I ran into her outside the motel this morning. She...she started pressing me. About Edward Dalton."

Matthew's expression didn't change, but the muscles in his jaw tensed. "What exactly did she say?"

Constantine hesitated, gathering the words carefully. "She thinks we're hiding something. She practically said it outright. Asked why I stopped short of Dalton's disappearance in my book. Like I left gaps on purpose."

Abigail shifted. Her voice was low but firm. "And what did you tell her?"

Constantine shook her head. "I told her I wrote what I could verify, nothing more. But she wouldn't let it go. She said people don't just vanish. Not without help."

The words landed like a weight between them, heavier than the quiet hum of the desk fan.

Matthew's face remained impassive, but his voice dropped a notch. "Did she mention Thomas?"

Constantine nodded. "She knows we've spent time together. I think she suspects I've told him more than I have. But Matthew, he's asking questions. And not just about Dalton. About the town. About us."

Abigail's arms tightened across her chest. "Thomas doesn't need to know everything. None of this was his fault. None of it was our fault. Like we've said before—"

"I know," Constantine interrupted, her voice tight. "But it's not just Thomas. Dr. Harper's determined. She told me her great-aunt was one of Dalton's victims. Someone he manipulated. She's not just here for research. This is personal for her. I don't think Thomas knows that information."

Matthew's brow furrowed, his hand pressing flat against the desk. "We can't undo what happened. Eldon made his choice. He carried that weight for the rest of his life. Digging it up now won't change anything. It'll just stir up pain."

Constantine looked between them, her voice quieter but no less insistent. "But isn't that what we're doing, hiding it? I care about Thomas and I'm trying to protect him, but I'm not sure I can if Dr. Harper keeps pushing."

Matthew's eyes darkened. "There's no body, Constantine. No evidence. No reason for anyone to dig deeper."

The silence stretched heavily, pressing against the walls of the small office.

Abigail finally spoke, softer now but no less firm. "Eldon never forgave himself for what happened that night. He carried that burden to his grave. And you know why we kept it quiet. It wasn't just for him. It was for all of us. For the people left behind who had to keep living here after Dalton disappeared. None of us know what she'll do with the truth."

Constantine's throat tightened. She knew she needed to keep it quiet. But knowing didn't make it easier to lie.

"I'm not saying we need to tell her everything," she whispered. "But if Thomas keeps pressing...I don't know if I can keep pretending I don't know the truth."

The floorboard creaked just outside the door.

Matthew's head snapped up, his sharp gaze shifting to the door as his hand hovered near the edge of his desk drawer. Abigail straightened, eyes narrowing toward the sound.

The clock ticked. The fan hummed.

No other noise followed.

After a beat, Matthew pushed back his chair, standing with slow, measured movements. He crossed the room, closed his hand around the brass doorknob, and twisted it open in one sharp motion.

The lobby beyond was empty.

The desk sat as they'd left it. The papers were neatly stacked. The coffee cup was untouched, its steam long faded. Sunlight stretched long across the floorboards.

Matthew scanned the space, eyes narrowing further, then exhaled quietly and shut the door.

"Thought I heard something."

Abigail's gaze lingered on the door. Her arms were still folded tightly. "You sure?"

He nodded once but didn't sit back down.

The quiet inside the office felt colder now.

Constantine finally broke the silence. "What do we do if she keeps pushing?"

Matthew's voice was low, measured, but unyielding. "We keep Eldon's secret. We stay quiet. We protect this family. The past stays buried, Constantine. That's the choice Eldon made, and *we* made when you wrote that book."

Constantine nodded slowly, but the unease hadn't left her.

Abigail spoke more gently now. "You're not alone in this. We'll watch Dr. Harper. If she digs too close—"

Matthew finished for her, voice hardening, "We'll send her in another direction."

Constantine knew, deep down, she wasn't sure how much longer she could keep pretending the truth didn't matter.

22

Beth Harper stood pressed against the wall just beyond view, heart pounding hard enough that she half-expected the sound to betray her.

She hadn't meant to listen. But she'd heard enough.

No body. No evidence. Let it stay buried.

The words clung to her thoughts, chilling and deliberate. The way the sheriff had spoken them, so carefully measured, so clearly rehearsed, only confirmed what Beth already suspected.

They were hiding something. And they would not tell her willingly. Not yet.

Beth's fingers curled tighter around her leather notebook, the worn cover pressing into her palm as she forced herself to steady her breath. She felt the cold press of the sheriff's office wall against her back, the scent of wood polish sharp and grounding, but her mind was racing.

She had been right to come here. To ask uncomfortable questions. Because someone in Puckerbrush knew the truth about Edward Dalton.

The tension in Constantine's voice earlier when she'd mentioned her book, her conversations with Thomas, it wasn't just discomfort. It was deflection.

She knew more. A lot more. And so did Matthew and Abigail Thompson.

Beth had seen Matthew's face just moments ago through the crack in the door. The sheriff's calm, almost practiced demeanor. Abigail standing stiffly by the ledgers, arms folded tight. The way Constantine's voice had dropped as if she was pleading for permission to tell the truth.

But they had all made their choice. Silence. A choice that only made Beth more certain they were protecting something. Or someone.

The words echoed again, sharper now. Heavier. Dalton hadn't just disappeared. She could feel it. *No body. No evidence. Let it stay buried.*

Beth exhaled slowly, forcing herself to ease back from the wall. Her pulse was finally slowing, but the fire beneath her ribs hadn't faded. She couldn't confront them yet. Not when they were this closed off. Not when Thomas was still caught in the middle.

The thought made her stomach twist with an uncomfortable tightness. He'd trusted Constantine too easily. Let his personal connection blind him to the fact that these people, this town, were not giving them the whole truth.

And yet, Beth couldn't shake the memory of how Constantine had looked at him. The way she had watched him at the café. Not as if she was manipulating him. But like she genuinely cared.

Which only made things more complicated.

Footsteps creaked faintly from the other side of the door. Beth froze.

The knob turned, and she pressed herself deeper into the shadows as the door cracked open.

Matthew Thompson's silhouette filled the frame, the afternoon sunlight spilling from the windows behind him, casting his face into shadow. He lingered there for a heartbeat too long, scanning the quiet lobby, his gaze sweeping the desk, the empty chairs. Looking for her.

Beth held her breath.

Finally, the door clicked shut.

The tension didn't ease. She knew exactly what had just happened. He had seen no one, but he had felt someone. And he was already on edge. She needed to be careful.

Drawing in a slow, controlled breath, Beth adjusted her grip on her notebook and slipped toward the side door, leaving the sheriff's office behind.

But she didn't feel relief as she stepped out onto the sunlit street.

Just the cold certainty that whatever had happened in Puckerbrush all those years ago, whatever Constantine, Matthew, and Abigail were protecting, she was closer than ever to uncovering. And they knew it, too.

23

Beth sat across from Thomas in the quietest corner of the Puckerbrush Café, her untouched coffee cooling beside her notebook. The space felt hushed now, the dinner crowd long gone, leaving only the clink of silverware in the kitchen and the soft murmur of conversation from a table near the window.

The silence was perfect. Controlled. And Beth knew how to use it.

Thomas was watching her, his posture guarded. Defensive, even. She could see it in the way his fingers flexed around the cup, the tension in his jaw as he waited for her to speak.

He was ready to defend Constantine. Which meant Beth needed to be careful.

She folded her hands on top of her notebook, choosing her words with the same precision she used when drafting her papers on historical gaps and forgotten truths.

"Thomas," she began, voice measured. "There's something I haven't told you yet. Something personal. And I think you deserve to know why I agreed to help you with this search in the first place."

His brow furrowed slightly, suspicion mingling with curiosity. "I thought you said it was the historical mystery about what happened to Dalton."

She nodded but held his gaze. "It was. But it's more than that. My great-aunt Donna was one of Edward Dalton's victims."

The words landed with quiet finality, their weight settling between them like a stone.

Thomas blinked, clearly surprised. He shifted back slightly in his chair, his grip easing on the cup. "I...I didn't know."

Beth allowed a breath to steady herself, though her pulse thrummed harder than she liked. She hadn't planned to share this part of her past. But it was the only way to break through his loyalty to Constantine.

"She was nineteen when Dalton came through her town. Small. Faithful. Not so different from Puckerbrush." Her voice softened, but she kept it even, factual. "Donna was desperate for hope. He promised miracles. He promised answers, and she believed him. She gave up everything she had for his ministry. Her trust. Her savings. Her faith. Herself."

She paused, the memory pressing heavier than she expected.

"And when the promises didn't come true, when he disappeared, it broke her. She never recovered. Not fully. And no one ever held him accountable. He just...vanished."

Thomas stayed quiet, absorbing her words. His face had softened, his defenses slipping, but she could see the conflict still there. The need to defend Constantine.

She forced herself to continue before he could retreat into that loyalty.

"That's why I took this case. When you asked me for help, I thought, if we could finally uncover the truth about Dalton's disappearance, it would mean something. Justice, in some small way. For Donna. For everyone he hurt."

Thomas nodded slowly, his face thoughtful now. But there was still hesitation in his silence.

And she knew it wasn't enough. Not yet. She leaned forward slightly, lowering her voice just enough to draw his focus back to her.

"But there's something else, Thomas. Something you need to hear."

His gaze snapped back to hers.

"I overheard Constantine earlier," she said, watching him closely. "She was with Matthew and Abigail at the sheriff's office. They were talking about Dalton. About...covering things up."

Thomas stiffened.

She pressed on, voice calm but direct. "They said, *'no body. No evidence. Let it stay buried.'* Those were their words, Thomas. I heard them with my own ears."

For a heartbeat, he didn't move. Then his hands tightened around the coffee cup, his knuckles pale.

"They're not just being cautious," Beth continued, careful to soften her tone. "They're hiding something. And Constantine...she's caught in it. I'm not saying she's lying to you, but she's protecting a truth she doesn't think you can handle."

His jaw clenched. She could see the turmoil now, written plainly on his face.

"Constantine told me everything she could," he said, but his voice lacked certainty. "She wrote about it in her book."

"But not what couldn't be proven," Beth interjected gently. "Think about it, Thomas. If Dalton just disappeared, no body, no trace, isn't it strange that everyone here seems so determined to keep it quiet? This town protects its stories. And it's protecting Constantine, too."

He shook his head slightly, gaze fixed on the window as if searching for answers beyond the café's lace curtains.

"I don't think she's lying," he whispered, almost to himself.

Beth didn't back off. She couldn't. Not when she was finally close to breaking through.

"I'm not saying she is," she whispered. "But she's afraid. Afraid of what digging too deep might uncover. Maybe even afraid for you."

His gaze returned to hers, conflicted. Searching.

"I just want you to ask yourself, why is she working so hard to stop you from asking these questions?"

Silence thickened between them.

Beth let the moment breathe, carefully gauging his reaction. His defenses weren't gone, but they were cracked. He believed her. Or at least, he was starting to. And that was enough. For now.

She reached for her notebook, flipping it shut with a quiet snap. "I'm going back to the museum later. There are still gaps in the town's records, things they didn't want on public display. If you're ready to stop relying on half-truths, you know where to find me."

Thomas nodded, but his mind was clearly somewhere else, the coffee forgotten between his hands.

Beth rose, smoothing the strap of her satchel over her shoulder. She'd planted the seed. Now, all she had to do was wait for the truth to break through. Because no matter how much Constantine Thornton wanted to keep the past buried,

It wouldn't stay hidden forever.

24

Three sharp raps on her motel room door made Constantine's heart stutter.

She knew it was Thomas before she even reached the door. The sinking feeling told her so.

When she opened it, the look on his face hit harder than the knock had. His eyes, usually so warm, were guarded now. Strained. Something had changed.

"Thomas?" Her voice felt too thin, too cautious. "What's wrong?"

He didn't step inside right away. Just stood there, fists clenched at his sides, jaw tight. "We need to talk."

The weight in his voice was unmistakable. For one brief, selfish moment, she wanted to pretend it was nothing. Some misunderstanding, something she could smooth over. But the ache behind his eyes told her differently.

She nodded, stepping back to let him in.

The room felt too quiet, the scent of her half-finished tea mingling with the dampness from the open window. The notebook on the table lay open to a blank page. She hadn't been able to write all evening. After her visit with Matthew and Abigail earlier, the words felt stuck.

Thomas stood just inside the door, arms crossed tightly like he was holding himself back. The silence stretched. Finally, he exhaled. "I talked to Dr. Harper."

Everything seemed to tilt slightly. Constantine's stomach tightened, the cold weight of inevitability pressing against her ribs.

"And?" she asked carefully. Too carefully.

His gaze was sharp, searching her face. "She told me about her great-aunt. Donna."

Constantine closed her eyes for a breath.

"I didn't know," he continued, voice softer now but no less tense. "Now I know why she was so eager to help me find answers." He paused as if he was just realizing the truth. "Donna trusted Dalton. He used her, and it destroyed her, Constantine. She was trying to tell me why this matters so much. Why we can't just...let it go."

Constantine nodded slowly, but the words she wanted to say wouldn't come. It wasn't the full reason Thomas was here. She could feel it. And when he spoke again, the ground beneath her seemed to shift.

"Dr. Harper overheard you," he said, voice dropping lower. "You. Matthew. Abigail. At the sheriff's office."

Her breath caught.

"She heard you talking about Dalton," he pressed on, eyes narrowing, pain threading into his voice now. "About keeping things buried. 'No body. No evidence. Let it stay buried.'"

The words felt like a physical blow, echoing back with the same finality Matthew had spoken them with. Her pulse hammered in her ears.

He knows. He knows I've been lying.

"Thomas—"

"Tell me the truth, Constantine." His voice cracked, raw. Desperate. "What does this mean? What aren't you telling me?"

She opened her mouth, the truth rising to the edge of her tongue, heavy and sharp. But she couldn't say it. Not all of it. Because if she told him. If she really told him. What then? Would he still look at her the same way? Would he still care for her once he knew the truth?

The truth was that Edward Dalton hadn't just disappeared. That her family—that she—was tied to that disappearance in ways she couldn't undo.

And if she didn't tell him? If she kept protecting this fragile, precious space where he still trusted her? How much longer could that lie hold before it fractured completely?

Her throat tightened. "I can't," she whispered, hating the words even as they left her lips.

Thomas stepped closer, his face etched with something she couldn't bear to see. Hurt. Disappointment.

"You can't?" he repeated, voice breaking. "Or you won't?"

She flinched.

"I'm trying to protect you, Thomas. You have to believe me."

"But from what?" His voice cracked, softer now, but no less fractured. "I trusted you, Constantine. I've trusted you with everything I've learned since I got here. And I thought—" His voice caught.

Don't say it, she begged silently.

"I thought you trusted me, too."

Her heart twisted painfully. "I do," she whispered, but it felt hollow when she couldn't give him what he was asking for.

The truth. The whole truth. But the truth would break everything. She could feel it, trembling beneath the surface of this fragile connection they'd built. So she didn't tell him. She folded her arms tightly across her chest, not in defiance but to hold herself together.

"Please, Thomas," she said, barely more than a whisper. "Trust me when I say some truths won't bring peace. They'll only cause more harm."

He stared at her for a long, silent moment. Searching. Waiting. And then, slowly, he shook his head.

"That's not good enough."

The words cut deeper than anything else he'd said. And when he turned toward the door, the angst rose so fiercely she almost called out to stop him. But she didn't. Because if she told him the truth, she was sure he wouldn't stay. This way, he was leaving, and she hadn't destroyed everything between them.

When the door clicked shut behind him, the silence left behind was almost unbearable.

25

The rain eased by morning, leaving the streets of Puckerbrush damp and quiet, the pale light of dawn barely cutting through the low-hanging mist. Thomas hadn't slept. The weight of Constantine's words, *I can't. Trust me,* echoed through his mind like a heartbeat, relentless and heavy. He'd spent half the night pacing his rented room, staring at the ceiling as though the answers he sought might appear there if he just looked hard enough.

Now, standing at the door of the Puckerbrush Museum, hands shoved deep in the pockets of his jacket, he wasn't sure what he was hoping to find.

The old bell above the door chimed softly as he entered, the scent of aged paper and wood polish thick in the air. Abigail Thompson glanced up from behind the worn oak counter where she'd been sorting a pile of yellowed newspapers. Her kind smile faded the moment she took in his face.

"Thomas." She set the papers aside, her voice quiet with concern. "You look...well, not yourself."

He forced a brittle half-smile, dragging a hand over his face. "Yeah. Rough night."

Abigail gestured to the stool across from her. "Come sit. Tell me what's going on."

He hesitated before sinking onto the stool, his fingers curling around the worn counter's edge as though anchoring himself. For a long moment, he said nothing. The quiet tick of the museum's grandfather clock filled the space between them.

Finally, he exhaled. "I talked to Constantine last night."

Abigail's expression shifted. It was softer now, more cautious.

"I confronted her," he continued, voice tight. "About what Dr. Harper overheard you discussing in Matthew's office. She told me about the words she heard, 'no body, no evidence, let it stay buried.'"

Abigail's eyes narrowed slightly. "So someone *was* there that day." Her lips pressed into a thin line. "I should have guessed it was her."

"She told me because she thought I deserved the truth," Thomas cut in, voice rough. "But Constantine...she wouldn't tell me anything. Just kept saying some truths would only bring more harm." His voice dropped lower. "I know she's keeping something from me. And I can't understand why."

Abigail studied him as if weighing how much to say. "She told you that directly?"

"Yes." His voice broke slightly. "I trusted her, Abigail. I thought she trusted me, too. Now I don't know what to believe."

The silence stretched, heavy as the mist clinging to the town outside.

Abigail folded her hands on the counter, voice measured. "You're right. Constantine *is* keeping something from you. And so am I."

His head snapped up, eyes narrowing. "You? Why?"

She sighed, the tension in her shoulders visible. "Because this... this isn't just about you, Thomas. Or even Constantine. It's about what people like Edward Dalton left behind. Along with the damage, and the secrets."

Thomas's jaw clenched. "Secrets? You're saying he...what? Hurt people? What did he do that was so terrible everyone wants to cover it up?"

Abigail met his gaze, steady but sad. "When I first came to

Puckerbrush, I wasn't supposed to stay. I was just covering for a friend on an article about the Centennial. But this town...it has a way of keeping people, of drawing you into its history." She paused. "I write mysteries, Thomas. And sometimes, I discover stories that are better left untouched."

Thomas's frown deepened, but he remained silent, waiting.

"I learned the truth about Matthew's family," Abigail continued quietly. "Matthew's father was adopted. His birth mother was Mary, Eldon's teenage daughter. And his father was Edward Dalton. When I uncovered that, it nearly destroyed him. Matthew's entire sense of identity unraveled. And yet, he forgave me. He made peace with it. But it took time. And pain."

She paused, voice softening further. "The truth can be brutal, Thomas. It doesn't just expose the past. It changes people. It breaks them. I'm telling you this because Constantine isn't just protecting herself. She's protecting her family. And, whether or not you see it, she's protecting you too."

The words landed like a blow to the chest.

Thomas shook his head, voice cracking. "Protecting me? From what? What could possibly be so awful that she can't trust me with it?"

Abigail exhaled slowly. "You're searching for answers because you think they'll give you peace. But what if they don't? What if knowing doesn't heal? What if it only deepens the wound?" She leaned in, her voice gentler now. "Edward Dalton hurt people. He left pain and regret trailing behind him, and that pain still lingers. The people who suffered because of him... they've found a way to move on. Maybe you need to consider doing the same."

The words hit him harder than he'd expected, like something tearing open inside him. He opened his mouth to speak, but nothing came.

"I just wanted the truth," he whispered finally, the fight draining from his voice.

Abigail's gaze softened. "I know. But the truth you're searching for won't undo the past. It won't change who your great-grandfather was.

And it won't undo the pain he caused. Especially not for Constantine."

Thomas's eyes dropped to the scuffed wooden floorboards, his pulse loud in his ears.

Silence pressed in again, deeper this time. He felt its weight settling heavily on his chest. No longer just anger. No longer betrayal. Something else now. Regret.

After a long beat, he nodded slowly and stood, the scrape of the stool against the old wood breaking the quiet. "Thank you, Abigail. For being honest with me. I need to think."

Abigail's lips curved in a sad, knowing smile. "Don't think too long, Thomas. Some things...some people...are worth fighting for. But not forever."

He nodded once more, then turned for the door, the soft chime of the bell ringing hollow in his ears as he left.

But the echo of her words lingered long after the door closed.

26

The warm scent of coffee and pastries lingered in the air of the Puckerbrush Café, mingling with the faint hum of conversation from a few scattered diners.

Thomas sat at the booth by the window, his fingers curling loosely around the ceramic mug in front of him. The coffee inside was still hot, steam curling upward in lazy spirals, but he hadn't taken a sip. Across the table, Beth's pen tapped softly against the edge of her notebook as she skimmed the map and photocopies spread between them.

"We're close," she said, the excitement in her voice subdued but unmistakable. "If we head a few towns east tomorrow, there's a good chance we'll find the missing pieces. Maybe even the final record of Edward Dalton's movements before Puckerbrush."

Thomas nodded absently, his gaze drifting out the window. Another town was just one more stop on the trail he'd been following for months. Another archive. Another lead.

And yet, for the first time, it didn't feel urgent. It didn't even feel important. The weight in his chest wasn't the pull of the past anymore; it was Constantine. The sound of her voice as she whispered, *I'm trying to protect you.* The way she had looked at him that last night, her expression filled with a sorrow that still haunted him.

"Thomas?" Beth's voice drew his attention back, her pen stilling as she glanced at him. "What are you thinking?"

He hesitated, his fingers tightening briefly around the mug before he set it down. "Beth," he said, his voice quieter than he intended. "I think I'm done."

Her brow furrowed, the words clearly catching her off guard. "Done? What do you mean? We're so close to figuring this out."

Thomas exhaled, leaning back against the worn cushions of the booth. "I know. But I've been thinking about this, about everything, and I'm wondering if finding out the full truth is really as important as I thought it was."

She tilted her head, the sharp curiosity he'd always admired in her flickering in her gaze. "What's changed?"

He paused, his eyes dropping to the papers between them, the edges worn from too much handling, pieces of a puzzle he wasn't sure he needed to finish anymore.

"Someone I care about has been carrying the truth of what happened for years," he began slowly, the words careful, deliberate. "And it hasn't brought her peace. It's only hurt her. She thought holding on to it would somehow make things right. That it was her responsibility to protect it, to protect me. And seeing that..." He shook his head, his chest tightening. "It's made me realize I don't want the same thing."

She leaned back, her expression softening.

"For a long time, I thought knowing everything about Edward Dalton, who he was, why he disappeared, would give me closure. That it would somehow make sense of the choices he made and how they shaped my family. But now I see it differently. The truth doesn't always heal. Sometimes it just hurts."

"And Constantine?" Beth asked gently.

Her name caught in his chest, the memory of her pale, guarded expression flashing through his mind. "She's carried so much she didn't have to. And I don't want to be the reason she keeps holding on to something that only weighs her down. I don't need to know more about Edward Dalton. Not if it costs us...whatever this is."

His voice faltered. The pressure in his chest became heavier before he took a steadying breath. "I'm letting it go," he said, his tone firm. "Because what matters to me now isn't Edward Dalton or his story. It's Constantine. And I can't keep chasing the past if it means losing her."

Beth studied him for a long moment, the lines of her face softening into quiet understanding. "So you've found your peace," she said.

He nodded. "I think I have. Knowing the full truth about Edward won't change the man I want to be. And it won't change what matters to me now."

He leaned forward, closing the folder of records they had been reviewing. The quiet snap of the clasp felt final in a way that surprised him, the tension in his chest easing slightly.

"I need to. This search has cost me personally. I need to decide where to go from here. I need to let Constantine know that I'm choosing her, not Edward Dalton. I'm going to go to her motel room and let her know what I've decided."

Her gaze softened further, a faint smile tugging at the corners of her mouth. "You've thought this through."

"I have."

The sound of rain tapping against the window filled the quiet between them, the café's warmth wrapping around them like a cocoon.

Finally, Beth reached for her coffee, lifting the mug with a quiet nod. "Good luck, Thomas," she said. "I hope you find what you're looking for. Some stories deserve to be told, but I understand why this one won't be."

"So do I," he murmured, his voice quiet but sure.

～

BETH STOOD outside the Puckerbrush Motel, the scent of fresh rain still lingering in the warming spring air. The late morning sun cast a soft golden hue over the damp pavement, glistening off the newly budding trees that lined the quiet streets. Somewhere in the distance, a bird trilled, its song breaking the hush that always followed a long rain.

Puckerbrush had given her more questions than answers.

She had come expecting to uncover history, but what she had found was something messier. Stories that weren't meant to be told, truths that weren't hers to claim.

For years, she had chased the shadow of Edward Dalton, determined to find closure. Not just for history's sake, but for her own. Aunt Donna had been one of the many women he had preyed upon, left behind with nothing but a broken faith and a child she hadn't been prepared to raise alone.

Her entire life, Beth had heard the whispered pain in her aunt's voice whenever his name was mentioned, had seen the way she flinched at the memory of those who blamed her instead of him. Dalton had stolen so much from her.

Beth had thought that exposing him, dragging his sins into the light, would bring justice. Would bring peace. But now, standing on the edge of the town that held his memories, she wasn't so sure.

Some stories deserved to be told. But some wounds ran so deep that the truth only risked reopening them.

She sighed, reaching into her pocket and pulling out her phone. After a brief hesitation, she composed a quick message:

Leaving town. If you ever decide you want to know more, you know how to find me.

She sent it to Thomas, then stared at the screen before navigating to her contacts and selecting another name. Aunt Donna.

Her thumb hovered over the call button. For years, she had believed that giving her aunt the full truth would make a difference. That knowing every painful detail about Dalton, his lies, his downfall, his death, would somehow ease the weight she carried.

But now? Maybe letting go was the better choice.

A soft breeze stirred the blooming lilacs beside the motel, their sweet scent drifting through the open car door as she slid behind the wheel. With one last glance at the fading *Welcome to Puckerbrush* sign in her rearview mirror, she pulled onto the road, the tires kicking up bits of damp gravel as she disappeared down the highway.

Her search in Puckerbrush didn't bring the answers she wanted for her aunt, but it did bring her information that would ease her pain a little.

27

P ale sunlight filtered through the gray morning sky as Constantine closed her suitcase with a quiet click. The scent of damp earth lingered outside her motel window, mist curling low across the fields like a veil.

She hadn't slept. Her chest felt heavier than the worn leather suitcase now resting on the bed, heavier than the words she hadn't said to Thomas the night before. *I can't. Trust me.*

But the truth was, she hadn't trusted him. Not completely. She'd chosen silence instead, and it had cost her.

She had told herself it was for his sake. That it was better to walk away than risk telling him the truth and watching the way his face might change, the way his eyes might dim with disappointment or hurt. But deep down, she knew the real reason.

She was protecting herself, too. Because she was falling in love with him. And love, real love, was terrifying.

She hadn't meant for it to happen. Hadn't wanted it to. It had been too soon, too unexpected, too much after the slow, inevitable ending of her relationship with Dave. She wasn't ready for something real, something that could hurt her if it fell apart.

And yet, Thomas had been different. His patience. His steady presence. The way he had looked at her like she was worth waiting for, like she was worth knowing, even when she kept pushing him away. And now she was pushing him away for good.

The motel room felt unbearably still. The half-empty cup of tea sat cold on the nightstand. A book she hadn't opened lay by the window, its pages untouched since their argument. She forced herself to take a steadying breath, smoothing her trembling hands over the faded cover of her suitcase as if the motion might steady her thoughts. It didn't.

The decision was made. Leaving was the only choice. If she stayed, she risked getting too close. Letting him in completely. Letting herself hope. And after everything with Dave, with the past, she wasn't sure she could survive losing again.

The only goodbye she'd offered was to Berta when she checked out that morning.

With her kind eyes and quiet wisdom, Berta had stood behind the motel's front desk and simply known. She hadn't pried, hadn't asked questions. She'd just taken Constantine's key, nodded, and said, "Take care of yourself, honey. You're always welcome back here. Remember that."

Now, behind the wheel of her car, the gravel crunched beneath her tires as she pulled onto the quiet road leading out of town.

The fields blurred by in shades of muted green and brown, but she barely noticed them. Her mind kept replaying the last time she'd seen Thomas. The rawness in his voice when he said, *I thought you trusted me, too.*

She pressed her lips together, blinking hard against the sting in her eyes.

It was better this way. It had to be. But if that were true, why did it feel like her chest was splitting open the farther she drove?

The drive home felt endless. By the time Constantine pulled into the driveway of her house, dusk had settled like a pale haze over the familiar landscape. The air smelled of damp pine and wood smoke, a stark contrast to the open fields of Puckerbrush.

But the house felt empty. No voices. No lingering scent of coffee. No warmth.

She dragged her suitcase inside and set it carefully in the hallway but made no move to unpack. Instead, she stood in the center of the quiet living room, arms wrapped tightly around herself, the silence pressing in on all sides.

The ticking of the clock above the mantel felt too loud.

The hollow ache wasn't going away.

Call Abigail.

The thought rose unbidden, and for a second, she resisted. Would Abigail be disappointed? Would she try to convince her to return?

But the loneliness settled too deeply, and she couldn't bear the quiet any longer.

With a shaky breath, she reached for her phone and pressed Call.

The line rang three times before Abigail picked up, her voice warm despite the static hum in the background.

"Constantine? Is everything okay?"

She swallowed hard, leaning against the back of the sofa. "I'm home."

A beat of silence. Then softer, gentler. "I see."

Constantine closed her eyes, the confession dragging out of her.

"I left this morning. I checked out of the motel. I couldn't stay. Not after last night. Not after...him."

Abigail didn't press. She didn't ask for explanations Constantine wasn't ready to give. Instead, her voice was calm. Reassuring. "You don't have to explain, Constantine. I get it."

Her chest tightened further. "Do you? Because right now, I don't think I do. I thought leaving would feel like the right thing. Like I was protecting everyone, but all I feel is—" Her voice caught. She pressed her fingers to her lips, fighting for control.

Abigail finished the sentence for her. "Like you left something unfinished."

Constantine nodded, though Abigail couldn't see.

"Yes." Her voice was barely more than a whisper.

Abigail let out a quiet sigh from the other end of the line. "Look, I'm not going to tell you how you should feel. But I will say this, you didn't leave to protect anyone, Constantine. You left because you're scared. And that's okay. But it doesn't mean you made the right choice."

The words hit harder than she expected.

Constantine blinked back the tears stinging her eyes. "It doesn't feel like I had another choice. I couldn't...I couldn't break his heart, Abigail. I couldn't risk what it might do to my family. What the truth might do to him? I may never see him again, but I know it's not because I shared a secret that drove him away."

Silence lingered, and she thought Abigail might finally say she agreed. That staying away was better.

But then, Abigail said, "Maybe you should let him decide that. Because all I see is two people hurting for no good reason other than fear."

The truth of it hurt. More than she was ready to admit.

She didn't respond. She couldn't.

Abigail's voice softened even further. "You don't have to figure this out tonight. Just... rest. And know that if you need me, I'm always here. Okay?"

Constantine nodded, whispering, "Okay. Thank you, Abigail."

They ended the call, and Constantine was left alone in silence again.

But somehow, it felt heavier now. Because, for the first time, she wasn't sure if she'd made the right choice at all.

28

Thomas parked his rental car outside the Puckerbrush Motel. The fields beyond the lot stretched pale and damp under the muted gray sky, the earth breathing softly after the storm.

He stepped out, the air cool against his skin, the scent of wet grass and lilacs clinging faintly to the breeze. Each step toward Constantine's door felt heavier than the last, but his resolve held firm.

He needed to tell her. He had decided. Edward Dalton's truth wasn't the only thing he had been searching for, after all. It was also Constantine. She had become the one thing he couldn't ignore, the one person who had made him see that the weight of the past wasn't worth losing what they could have together. He needed to tell her he was falling in love with her.

Stopping in front of her door, he raised his hand to knock, the faint echo of their last conversation still pressing against his chest. *I'm trying to protect you.*

Not anymore.

He knocked once, twice, his heart pounding harder with each passing second of silence. Finally, he stepped back, glancing around the empty lot, confusion creeping in.

Where was she?

Thomas knocked again, louder this time, but the only response was the faint rustling of leaves from the trees at the edge of the property. His chest tightened, unease threading through his thoughts as he stepped closer to the window, peering through the thin curtain.

The room was empty. The bed was made, the surfaces cleared. Only the faint impression of a life recently lived, lingered.

She was gone.

Thomas's breath caught, his fists clenching at his sides as the realization settled over him like the mist clinging to the fields. She had left.

The weight of the moment bore down on him, heavy and cold. He turned back to his car, his movements slower now, his mind racing as he tried to piece together what had happened. Had she decided he wasn't worth the risk? That whatever secret she was protecting was too great to share?

The questions pressed against his ribs as he slid into the driver's seat, gripping the wheel tightly. He stared out at the empty lot, the rain-softened gravel blurring through his unfocused gaze.

She hadn't just left the motel. She had left him.

Thomas found himself parked outside Abigail and Matthew's farmhouse. The wooden porch stretched before him, the soft glow of light spilling from the windows casting long shadows across the damp grass.

Abigail answered the door almost immediately, her sharp eyes narrowing slightly when she saw him. "Thomas?"

He stepped inside without waiting for an invitation, his movements brisk but not unkind. "She's gone."

Abigail's brow furrowed. "Gone?"

"Constantine," he said, his voice rougher now. "She's left. She's not at the motel."

Abigail's shoulders relaxed slightly, though her gaze remained steady. "She called me this morning," she admitted after a moment. "She left for the city. She said little, just that she needed time."

Thomas exhaled, the tightness in his chest shifting into something sharper, an ache that felt like regret. "She didn't tell me."

"No," Abigail whispered. "She didn't."

He ran a hand through his hair, pacing a short line near the edge of the kitchen table. "I came here to tell her I'm done with the search. I wanted her to know...she's more important to me than any of this. Edward Dalton's past, the truth—it doesn't matter anymore. But I can't tell her if she's already gone."

Abigail watched him quietly, her gaze thoughtful. "She left because she thinks she's protecting you, Thomas. You know that, don't you?"

He stopped pacing, turning to face her fully. "Protecting me from what? The truth? I don't care about her family's or my family's past, Abigail. I care about her. But she's so convinced that what she's hiding will change everything."

Stepping closer, Abigail's voice was soft but firm. "She's carrying more than just a secret, Thomas. She's carrying guilt. She's afraid of what you'll think, not just about the truth, but about her for keeping it. She's been running from this for a long time."

Thomas's chest tightened further, his voice breaking slightly as he replied. "I just...I don't want her to think she's alone in this."

"Then go to her, Thomas," Abigail said. "If you care about her, show her. But first, give her time."

Her words hit hard, cutting through the frustration and confusion clouding his thoughts.

He said nothing, the faint crackle of the fire in the background filling the silence. Then, finally, he nodded, his hands settling firmly at his sides.

"I'll give her time," he whispered. "Then I'll find her."

Abigail smiled faintly, a warmth in her gaze that felt like quiet approval. "Good. She'll realize she needs you, Thomas. Even if she doesn't know how to say it."

He didn't hesitate this time, turning back toward the door with renewed purpose. The rain had stopped, but the air still smelled of damp earth and lilacs as he stepped outside.

The road ahead felt wide and uncertain, but for the first time, the weight in his chest shifted.

29

The rain had come and gone, leaving the scent of damp earth lingering in the cool morning air. Outside, the dogwood tree in the yard had burst fully into bloom, its delicate white petals drifting gently to the ground with each passing breeze. For the first time in a week, Constantine noticed.

She sat curled on the sofa, the soft weight of a blanket draped over her legs, watching the sunlight filter pale and golden through the mist still clinging to the glass. The house felt quieter than usual but not as heavy. Not as lonely.

A cream-colored envelope lay open on the coffee table, Abigail's unmistakable looping script across the front. She'd only read the invitation once, but the words had stayed with her.

Please join us for a Baby Shower Honoring Lydia Piper. Saturday, 2 p.m. at the Puckerbrush Community Hall.

There was something so simple, so warm about it. No expectation. No pressure. Just an invitation from a friend who hadn't stopped thinking of her. Puckerbrush.

It had been a few weeks since she left, since she closed the motel door behind her and pressed the room key into Berta's hand with a quiet goodbye. She hadn't even unpacked when she returned home, her suitcase still half-full in the corner where she'd left it, as if part of her wasn't sure whether she was really supposed to stay.

But now, as she traced the curve of Abigail's signature with her thumb, she felt something else stirring. A pull. Not just toward the town, but the people she'd left behind.

She missed them.

She missed belonging somewhere. The realization settled deep in her center. It was softer than the ache she'd grown so used to carrying.

Not that she didn't think of Thomas. Of course, she did. She felt his absence in ways she hadn't expected, in quiet moments when the house felt too still or when the scent of rain caught her off guard, reminding her of that last night in Puckerbrush. But he was gone now. She knew that.

The questions that had brought him to town were answered as best they could be. His great-grandfather's story, at least the version she could give him, was complete. He had no reason to return. And maybe that was for the best.

Constantine exhaled, pushing the blanket aside as she stood. The unease pressure was still there, but it wasn't as sharp today. It wasn't as loud.

She reached for the invitation once more, smoothing the edges where her thumb had pressed too hard.

She was going back to Puckerbrush. But to be part of something again, and for the first time in a long while, that felt good.

As the town came into view a few days later, she realized just how much she'd missed this place. The quiet charm of it all, the way the town seemed to exist in its own rhythm, untouched by the outside world.

The ache hadn't vanished entirely, but it no longer felt like a weight pressing against her ribs. Not today. Today felt lighter.

She thought of Abigail and Lydia, of Martha's teasing humor and Emily's calm presence. The people she cared about in ways she hadn't expected. And Berta. Steady, reliable Berta had become more than just the friendly face behind a motel counter.

Abigail told her Thomas had left. His search for answers had ended. His questions, at least the ones she could answer, had been resolved. And that was good. It was. Her guilt of not being able to tell him the truth had eased.

The gravel crunched softly beneath her tires as she turned into the lot of the Puckerbrush Motel. The potted geraniums on the porch were already in full bloom, their bright red petals vivid against the pale blue trim. The old neon sign, *Puckerbrush Motel—Vacancy*, still hung slightly crooked.

It looked exactly the same. Steady. Familiar. And this time, so did the feeling it stirred inside her. Home.

Constantine cut the engine but lingered a short time. The town pressed in around her, quiet and expectant but not in the heavy way she'd felt before.

This time, she wanted to be here. She wasn't running from anything. She wasn't hiding. She was returning to the people who had made this place feel like home.

The bell above the door chimed softly as she stepped inside, the scent of lemon polish and old wood welcoming her back with open arms.

Berta looked up from behind the counter, reading glasses perched low on her nose, a half-finished crossword puzzle spread across the desk in front of her. The moment her eyes landed on Constantine, her entire face shifted, softening with something warmer than surprise.

"Well, look who's come back," Berta said, setting her pencil aside with a smile that made Constantine's throat tighten in ways she hadn't expected.

The knot in her chest loosened further as she returned the smile. "Hey, Berta."

Berta took her in for a moment, head tilting as if measuring something unsaid, then folded her hands on the counter.

"You okay, honey?"

Constantine opened her mouth but hesitated. What was there to say, really? She had expected this. The ease of it all. The warmth. The kindness.

"I am now," she answered honestly, her voice quieter than she intended but no longer carrying the heaviness it had once had.

Berta's expression gentled. "Abigail said you'd be coming for Lydia's shower. I'm glad you did. Lydia will be, too."

Constantine nodded, her fingers brushing the strap of her bag where it rested against her shoulder. She had expected it to feel natural. While the ache hadn't disappeared entirely, it no longer felt so sharp.

Berta reached behind the counter, retrieving the same brass key Constantine had used every visit before, sliding it gently across the worn wood.

"Room eight. Kept it ready for you."

Constantine took the key, the familiar weight of it grounding her which she didn't realized she needed.

"Thanks, Berta."

Berta's smile softened further, a quiet reassurance behind it.

"Welcome home, Constantine."

The room was exactly as she remembered.

The lavender sachet still tucked neatly behind the pillows. The quilt folded at the foot of the bed, floral curtains filtering the afternoon light into soft patterns along the wall. It was familiar. Safe. The silence felt like peace, not waiting.

Constantine set her suitcase on the bed, gently running her fingers over the quilt's edge before turning toward the window.

The mist had lifted now, revealing the fields beyond the edge of town. The rain was gone. The sky was brighter, the first hints of sunset painting the horizon.

She hadn't allowed herself to think of Thomas much during the drive here, but now, as the quiet settled around her, she felt his absence in a way she couldn't quite shake. Not painful. Just...there.

But this wasn't about him. Tomorrow was about Lydia. About

celebration. About showing up for the people who had been there when she needed them most.

She could do this. She would do this.

And since leaving, Constantine felt like maybe she was returning to herself.

30

Warm sunshine lingered on her skin as a gentle breeze stirred the scent of lilacs in the air. The sky stretched wide and clear, the pale spring blue that made everything feel a little softer, a little more alive.

Ahead, the Puckerbrush Community Hall stood just beyond the garden, the sunlight catching the white clapboard siding, making the windows glint.

She hadn't expected her hands to shake. It was just a baby shower. A celebration.

And yet, as she adjusted the strap of the gift bag and smoothed the skirt of her dress, the pressure against her ribs felt heavier than it should have.

The voices drifting through the hall's open windows carried easily. There was laughter, the warm hum of conversation, the sound of life being shared.

She could do this for Lydia and for Abigail. For a town that, despite the distance she had put between herself and Puckerbrush, still felt like home.

The door opened before she could knock, and Abigail appeared, sunlight catching the strands of her hair as her face lit up with a familiar, genuine smile.

"Constantine! You made it."

Before Constantine could respond, Abigail was already pulling her into a hug, its warmth steady and grounding. Lavender and something faintly sweet lingered on her sweater, the scent so familiar it nearly undid her.

When they pulled apart, Abigail kept her hands on Constantine's arms a moment longer, searching her face with the quiet care of someone who noticed everything but never pressed too hard.

"I'm glad you're here," she breathed.

Constantine nodded, the lump in her throat making words feel difficult. "I wouldn't miss it."

And somehow, as the sunlight streamed in behind them, it felt true.

The community hall was bright and alive. Sunlight poured through the wide windows, spilling golden light across the wooden floors. Pale blue and pink ribbons draped along the windowsills, catching the breeze that stirred the lace curtains. A long table near the center of the room was arranged with delicate sandwiches, sugared pastries, and a cake adorned with fresh berries and edible flowers.

A smaller table near the back overflowed with gifts. There was floral wrapping paper and ribbons tied in perfect bows, each one carefully placed with the same thoughtfulness Constantine expected from this town.

Lydia stood near the windows, glowing in a soft yellow dress that skimmed over the gentle curve of her belly. She was speaking with a few women Constantine didn't recognize. Nurses, probably coworkers, judging by their conversations drifting through the room.

And near her sat Penelope, Lydia's grandmother, watching everything with quiet pride, her hands folded delicately in her lap, her eyes sharper than her soft smile suggested.

Martha and Emily worked near the food table, arranging platters and fussing over the cake with a quiet, practiced rhythm. Berta stood near the table, arranging a fresh vase of flowers, her face lighting up the moment she spotted Constantine. Without a word, she crossed the room, her arms already outstretched.

"There's my girl," Berta whispered, wrapping Constantine in a hug.

It wasn't the decorations or the careful planning that struck her most. It was the warmth. The way every conversation seemed touched with laughter. The way people greeted each other not out of politeness but out of genuine affection. The way it felt like family.

Lydia was next to notice her.

"Constantine!" Her face lit up, and she crossed the room with that same gentle grace, one hand resting over her belly, the other reaching for Constantine's as she approached.

Her pulse caught as she handed over the gift, her voice softer than she'd intended. "Congratulations, Lydia. I'm so happy for you."

Lydia took the bag carefully, her fingers lingering as she held it close.

"Thank you," she whispered, her voice thick with quiet emotion. "It means a lot that you're here."

Constantine nodded, words feeling too small for the knot forming in her throat.

Penelope's voice drifted toward them from across the room, the words quiet but clear. "I'm glad you could make it."

"Me too." Constantine met the older woman's gaze, and for the first time, she didn't feel measured under the weight of it.

The afternoon passed in waves of quiet joy. Laughter rippled easily through the room, rising and falling like music.

"Absolutely not," Lydia said, laughing as Martha held up a baby name book, her finger resting on a page.

"What's wrong with *Horace* or *Ethel*?" Martha teased, arching a brow.

"It sounds like he or she was born already eighty," Lydia said, wrinkling her nose as a few of the women chuckled. "Besides, it reminds me of that rooster we had growing up. The one that chased me around the yard."

Listening from her chair by the window, Penelope gave a quiet smile. "That rooster was a menace, but to be fair, you tried to dress him in a doll bonnet once."

The room erupted with laughter, and the sound settled warmly in Constantine's chest, easing something she hadn't realized had been so tight.

Emily raised her phone just as Lydia unwrapped a pair of tiny, knitted booties.

"Hold those up again," she said with a grin, snapping a picture. "That's going in the album."

Lydia rolled her eyes affectionately but held up the booties, anyway.

Standing near the gift table, Berta chuckled softly. "I remember when my mama made a pair just like those for my little brother. He outgrew them before he even got to wear them."

"Babies tend to do that," Martha added, leaning in with a conspiratorial smile. "Which is why we're all here to spoil you rotten with enough onesies for an entire army."

The teasing, the shared stories, the unspoken love woven into every exchange. It filled the room and made the sunlight feel warmer somehow.

Constantine stayed near the edges, watching. Not out of discomfort but because it was enough. Enough to witness this kindness. To see how these women, this town, held each other close. Enough to feel, for the first time in far too long, like she was part of it.

Later, as the last gifts were opened, and the cake was shared, the noise softened into quiet conversation.

The scent of lilacs drifted in from the garden as the sun dipped lower, streaking the floorboards with a golden glow.

Constantine stood by the open window, letting the breeze brush against her skin, the air soft with the promise of spring.

The ache she'd carried since arriving felt lighter now as if it had been folded into the laughter that still lingered in the room.

Abigail appeared beside her, the ribbon from one gift tied loosely around her wrist.

They just stood there, side by side, watching Penelope gently help Lydia gather the opened presents while Berta refilled lemonade glasses.

Constantine hesitated, then whispered, "Thank you."

Abigail turned slightly, brow lifting. "For what?"

Constantine exhaled, her fingers tracing the hem of her sleeve. "For inviting me. For reminding me it's...it's okay to be here."

Abigail's expression softened. Her voice was gentle but steady. "Constantine, you never left us. You just needed time to find your way back. We're always here for you."

The words pressed deeper than they should have, leaving her feeling a little lighter.

31

Thomas hadn't realized how much he'd missed the scent of pine and rain-soaked earth until he crossed into Puckerbrush.

The sun hung bright and steady in the pale blue sky. The town stretched quietly beneath it, the damp scent of spring blossoms lingering in the air. It looked the same, and yet, everything felt different.

A few weeks had passed. A few weeks since he'd packed his bags, driven back to Fairview, and tried to lose himself in work, hoping time and distance would dull the ache in his chest.

It hadn't. Not when the questions followed him. Not when she followed him. Constantine's face pressing into his mind in quiet moments, her voice echoing that single, fractured truth. *I thought you trusted me, too.*

He gripped the steering wheel tighter as he pulled into the parking lot of the Puckerbrush Motel, the gravel crunching softly beneath him.

The geraniums on the porch still bloomed brightly in their terra-cotta pots. The neon sign, *Puckerbrush Motel—Vacancy*, hung slightly crooked just as before. But this time, there was something new. A sign taped carefully to the front door.

CLOSED UNTIL 4 P.M.
Join me at Lydia Piper's Baby Shower!
Berta

Thomas stared at it for a long moment. Of course, Berta was there. She'd always been part of the fabric of this town, the person who showed up for everyone.

And Constantine...she was there too. He knew it. He exhaled, tension pressing deeper between his ribs. The ache had never really been about the town or his family's past. It had always been about her.

The motel was quiet without Berta's presence. The silence felt heavier than it should have, pressing against his chest as he stood in the empty parking lot.

He could still leave. He could turn around and drive back to Fairview and forget this town. Forget her.

But the ache wasn't letting go, and if he didn't face it now, if he didn't see *her*, he wasn't sure it ever would.

Thomas stood there for another breath before turning back toward the car.

He knew where the community hall was. He knew who he was really going there for. And this time, he wasn't leaving without answers.

The drive from the motel to the community hall wasn't long. Barely five minutes. But with every turn, the tension in Thomas's chest seemed to ratchet tighter. The sun streamed through the trees, dappling the narrow road with shifting patterns of light and shadow. The grass sparkled with raindrops from the morning rain, but he barely noticed. His hands tightened around the wheel. His knuckles pale as the hall came into view at the top of the hill.

The whitewashed building stood as it always had, simple and welcoming, with tall windows thrown open to let in the warm spring air. Pink and blue streamers fluttered gently along the porch railing, and a few cars were parked neatly along the gravel shoulder. Constantine's was one of them. He could hear the soft hum of conversation, occasional bursts of laughter carrying on the breeze, but the sound only made the pain behind his ribs press harder.

He pulled into a spot at the far edge of the lot but didn't turn off the engine. The rumble beneath his hands was steady, familiar, but nothing inside him felt steady now. The longer he sat there, the worse it became. Unsaid words weighing heavy on his chest, memories pressing closer.

He could pretend none of this mattered. Pretend that seeing Constantine again wouldn't tear something open inside. But that was a lie, wasn't it?

It mattered. More than he'd admitted, even to himself.

He thought he'd left Puckerbrush to close the door on his great-grandfather's past, but the truth, the uncomfortable, undeniable truth, was that leaving Constantine had felt like a fracture he didn't know how to mend. And now, he wasn't sure if he'd come back to make peace with the past or to figure out if there was something still between them.

He exhaled and let his head fall back against the headrest, eyes closing for a beat. Then he saw her. A glimpse of the far side of the hall, just beyond the window.

The dark sweep of her hair, the familiar way she tilted her head when she laughed.

The sound didn't quite reach him, but it didn't have to. The sight alone knocked the breath from his lungs.

For a second, he considered starting the car again. But he didn't. Because no matter how far he'd driven from this town, she had never really left him.

The engine went silent as he pushed the button. The absence of sound felt louder somehow, pressing against his chest. His pulse hammered as he stepped out of the car, the warm breeze brushing against his face. It wasn't too late. It couldn't be. Not yet.

The gravel shifted beneath Thomas's boots as he made his way toward the hall's entrance, each step feeling heavier than it should. The soft scent of lilacs clung to the air, mingling with the damp earth and sunlight as a breeze stirred the pale ribbons tied along the porch railing. The quiet hum of conversation blended with the occasional burst of laughter that drifted through the open windows.

Abigail's unmistakable voice.

Martha teasing someone, her laugh rising above the others.

And then there was Constantine.

He hadn't heard her voice yet, but he didn't need to. The awareness of her presence was already there, as steady and undeniable as the pressure against his ribs.

He stood at the bottom step, staring at the open door.

He could leave before anyone noticed, before she saw him, and return to Fairview, where things were simpler. Where his life hadn't been tangled with hers in a way he still didn't fully understand. But leaving hadn't made the ache disappear before, and it wouldn't now. Not when she was just beyond that door.

His hand brushed the porch railing as he climbed the steps, the worn wood warm beneath his fingertips. Sunlight caught the edges of the blue and pink streamers, filling the space with a soft golden glow. The scent of cake and cut flowers drifted toward him as he reached for the door.

And then he saw her. She stood near the far window, half-turned, a glass of lemonade held lightly in her hand. The sunlight seemed drawn to her, catching in the dark waves of her hair, tracing the soft curve of her profile. She was listening to Abigail, nodding slowly, her expression calm but guarded in a way that twisted something deeper inside him.

She looked peaceful.

Or maybe she was just better at hiding the ache than he was.

The door creaked softly as it swung wider beneath his hand, and a few heads turned, drawn by the sound. He felt the weight of their attention, but it was distant, muffled beneath the steady thrum of his pulse.

Abigail noticed him first. Her gaze lifted, brow arching slightly, surprise flashing across her face before it softened into something gentler, more knowing. She didn't speak, but her small nod felt like permission, as if she understood exactly why he was there.

Standing near the dessert table with a plate of cake balanced carefully in one hand, Berta turned next. Her lips parted, eyes widening just a fraction, but she said nothing either.

And then Constantine turned. Their eyes met.

The noise, the warmth of the room, the scent of lilacs and cake— it all faded, dimming beneath the sudden, heavy press of that single shared glance.

Her expression shifted, the softness giving way to something more uncertain, her lips parting as if she might speak, but the words never came.

Neither of them moved. Neither of them spoke.

And in that charged silent moment, Thomas felt it all over again. The ache, the questions, the unbearable weight of everything they hadn't said.

32

Surrounded by the joyous chaos of Lydia's baby shower, Constantine felt lighter, almost happy.

Being back in Puckerbrush was easier than she'd expected. Familiar faces, warm smiles, the comfort she'd been missing without realizing it.

And yet, all of that steadiness shifted the moment she saw him. Half-shadowed, he stood just inside the doorway, yet her eyes instantly found him.

The breath caught in her throat.

He looked...good. Different, but not in a way that spoke of distance. If anything, it was the way his gaze softened when it met hers. He seemed tentative, searching, as if he wasn't sure he should be there but had come anyway. For her.

Her fingers tightened around the glass of lemonade in her hand, heart thudding which she hadn't prepared for.

She'd told herself he wouldn't come back. That his questions had been answered. That he had no reason to return. And yet, here he was.

And she wasn't sure what startled her more, the angst that stirred at the sight of him, or the flicker of quiet hope beneath it.

For a long moment, neither of them moved.

Martha's laughter drifted from the corner where Lydia was holding up a pair of impossibly tiny baby socks, but Constantine barely heard it. Everything else, the gifts, the cake, the cheerful chatter, faded into background noise as Thomas took a single step closer. And then another.

"Thomas." Her voice was softer than she intended, but his name felt familiar on her lips, like something she'd held back for too long.

His posture eased just slightly, the tension in his shoulders releasing as his gaze met hers fully. "Hey."

The sound of his voice, quiet and steady, made her heart stutter. He was really here. And she couldn't help but wonder, was he here for her?

He hesitated, glancing around the room as if suddenly aware he didn't quite belong. The handful of women still mingling near the dessert table hadn't noticed him yet. They were too busy helping Lydia collect the last of the opened gifts. Still, his focus returned to Constantine.

"I didn't mean to interrupt," he said, his voice softer now. "I just...I heard about the shower. I wanted to be here."

She swallowed hard, her chest tightening as warmth spread low in her stomach. For a heartbeat, she wanted to believe it was just about the shower.

But the way he looked at her, like she was the only person in the room who mattered, told her otherwise.

"I'm glad you're here," she admitted, voice quieter but steady. "Lydia will be happy to see you."

They both knew that wasn't why he was here.

The silence between them shifted. Not uncomfortable, just heavy with things unsaid.

His eyes searched hers, lingering, as if waiting for permission to say something more.

"How have you been, Constantine?"

Her lips parted, but the words tangled somewhere deep inside her. How was she supposed to answer that? She'd missed him. She'd thought about him every day since she left. But the fact that she was afraid of what he'd think of her if he learned the truth was a weight she still couldn't find the courage to share. So she settled for the easier version.

"I've been good." A lie, and they both knew it. She forced a small smile, brushing a loose strand of hair behind her ear. "Keeping busy."

His expression softened, but his eyes didn't leave hers.

"I've been trying to do the same," he admitted. His voice was quieter now, like he wasn't sure how much to reveal. "But it hasn't been easy. Not when I—"

"Thomas."

Her voice caught, too fragile, too raw. She shook her head, taking a half step back. "Not here. Not today."

The pain was harder, the weight of everything they weren't saying hanging heavy between them. "I can't do this. Not right now."

The pain in his face was subtle but unmistakable. He nodded, the muscle in his jaw tightening before he spoke again.

"I get it. I do."

She could see it. The struggle to hold back, the questions still lingering behind his eyes. But he didn't press. And maybe that was what hurt most of all.

Because a part of her, despite everything, wanted him to stay.

The sound of wrapping paper crinkling drew both their attention as Lydia lifted the last gift from the table, a beautifully wrapped box with a pale pink ribbon.

The moment between them shifted, the soft chatter rising again as the celebration continued. But the ache remained.

Constantine returned to the window, watching the late afternoon sun spill in golden streaks across the wooden floorboards, her heart still thudding a little too fast.

She twisted around to see Thomas, still near the doorway, lingering as if he wasn't quite ready to leave. And neither was she.

33

The ache hadn't eased. It only deepened, pressing heavier.

Not here. Not today. The weight of her words lingered in his head as he watched Constantine move back to the group gathered around Lydia.

She hadn't rejected him. Not really. But the way she'd said it, the way her voice trembled just enough to catch. He felt it. The wall she'd built was still there, and he hadn't been able to break through. Not yet.

Thomas exhaled slowly, raking a hand through his hair as his gaze drifted over the room.

Berta was chatting with Penelope now, her face animated as she gestured toward the empty cake platter, probably offering to bring out more. Martha helped Lydia collect the last of the wrapping paper while Abigail stood near the gift table, folding tissue paper with that effortless grace she always carried.

Everyone else looked at ease. Like they belonged here. But he didn't. Not today. Not when the ache felt so loud, so unresolved.

He'd come back to Puckerbrush thinking it would be simple. Thinking time and distance would have made it easier to see her, to speak the words that had tangled inside him since he left.

But seeing her again, hearing her voice, watching the way her eyes had softened and yet still held him at arm's length made everything feel harder. Because he knew she was protecting herself or protecting him. And he wasn't sure which was worse.

The sound of chairs scraping back pulled him from his thoughts.

The guests were drifting toward the door now, lingering in small groups as the shower wound down. Penelope was hugging Lydia, whispering something that made her granddaughter smile while Berta packed leftovers into neatly labeled containers.

Thomas caught sight of Constantine again near the far table, standing slightly apart from the others, speaking quietly with Emily. Her arms were folded loosely, her face calm, but he saw it. The way her fingers pressed against her sleeve, fidgeting, tense.

She wasn't as calm as she wanted everyone to believe. And neither was he.

Abigail approached him. Her expression was gentle as she stepped to his side. "She's not avoiding you," she whispered, without preamble.

Torn between frustration and gratitude that she could read him so clearly, Thomas blinked. "Could've fooled me."

"She's being careful," Abigail continued, her voice steady. "That's not the same thing."

He shook his head, gaze still on Constantine as she nodded at something Emily said, her smile small but polite, just enough to be convincing.

"She didn't trust me enough to be honest," he said. "I came back for answers, Abigail. And she's still keeping me out."

Abigail's expression shifted, her gaze softening as she tilted her head toward him. "You're not giving her enough credit. Constantine isn't keeping you out. She's trying not to break you. And herself."

Thomas frowned. "What does that even mean?"

She sighed, folding her arms as she glanced toward the window, her voice more careful now. "You know how much she loves this town. She'd do anything to protect the people she cares about, even when it hurts her in the process. And you...*you* are one of those people, Thomas."

His throat tightened, a bitter edge creeping into his voice. "Then why does it feel like she's shutting me out? If she cared, she wouldn't keep pushing me away."

Abigail's gaze returned to his, steady. "Because she's afraid. And you're afraid too, whether you want to admit it or not."

The words settled deep, uncomfortable in their truth. He was afraid. Afraid of being hurt again. Afraid of hearing the truth he'd been chasing since the day he arrived in Puckerbrush. About his great-grandfather, about Constantine's family, about why she'd let him leave without a fight.

But mostly, he was afraid of what would happen if he stayed. If there was no closure to be found. If he had to face the fact that some things, some people, couldn't be fixed.

The crowd had thinned even more now.

Constantine was helping Lydia gather the last of the gifts, her back half-turned. She hadn't looked his way since their conversation.

And maybe that was for the best. Because despite everything pressing inside him, despite the ache that still hadn't eased, he couldn't push her today. But he wasn't leaving, either. Not this time.

34

The last of the guests had drifted out, leaving behind the lingering scent of lilacs and cake. Sunlight slanted low across the community center's floor, painting lacework shadows from the curtains onto the worn wood.

Constantine stood by the window, arms wrapped around herself, watching the quiet street outside. She could feel Thomas's presence behind her, the way his gaze hadn't left her. He hadn't spoken, hadn't tried to press her again. Not yet. But the weight of all they hadn't said sat heavily between them.

She wanted to leave, to escape the pain pressing against her chest, but her feet stayed rooted. Because the truth wouldn't leave her alone.

The truth was that Eldon, her great-great-uncle, was the reason Thomas's great-grandfather, Edward Dalton, disappeared from Puckerbrush all those years ago. And Thomas had no idea.

She had buried it, kept the truth locked away when she wrote her book, convinced that some secrets belonged to the past. But now, standing in the hush of this quiet place, with Thomas so close and so patient, it felt heavier than ever. And he deserved to know.

If she told him, if she shattered the image of the man he'd been searching for, would he walk away? Would he look at her and not see the woman he had trusted, but the descendant of a killer?

The creak of the wooden floor snapped her out of her spiraling thoughts.

"Constantine."

His voice was gentle. No accusations. Just her name.

She turned slowly, firming her expression and meeting his gaze with a sense of wariness.

"I thought you'd be gone by now," she said.

Thomas shook his head, stepping closer but keeping his hands firmly in his pockets. "I thought about it. But I didn't want to leave like this."

She swallowed, turning back to the window as if she could somehow will the words she wanted to say into existence. "Thomas... I'm trying to protect you. That's all I've ever tried to do."

"Protect me from what?" His voice softened, but the quiet insistence in it made her throat tighten.

"You wouldn't understand."

He exhaled, stepping closer still, his voice low but steady. "Then help me understand, Constantine. Because from where I'm standing, it feels like you're pushing me away. Keeping me at a distance for reasons you won't let me see."

She shook her head, heart pounding harder against her ribs. "It's not that simple—"

"Yes, it is," he interrupted gently. "You're afraid of something. And I need you to trust me enough to let me in."

The truth pressed hard against her chest. *My great-great uncle killed your great-grandfather.* The words rose and almost broke free. But the cost felt unbearable.

So instead, she whispered, "I don't want to lose you, Thomas."

He blinked, startled by the rawness in her voice. "You're not going to lose me. But you're shutting me out, Constantine. And whatever you're protecting me from, it's hurting you."

A tear slipped free despite her efforts to keep her composure. She brushed it away quickly, shaking her head. "You don't know what you're asking. If I tell you, it won't just hurt you. It will change how you see everything. Your family and me."

His brow furrowed. "You're not responsible for what happened in the past. And you're not responsible for my family's past. And I can't keep standing on the outside of whatever this is. You have to let me in."

Her chest tightened. The pain was unbearable. How could she explain it? How could she tell him about the man his family had praised for generations? That her own blood had buried the preacher who disappeared without a trace, here in this town.

"Thomas, I don't know how to do this," she whispered.

He took a small step closer, his voice softer now, more vulnerable. "Do what?"

"Tell you the truth without losing you."

His face softened, but she could see the flicker of pain there, too. The hurt in not knowing why she was holding back.

"You won't lose me." His voice was barely above a whisper now. "Whatever it is...we can face it together."

She shook her head, blinking back tears. "You say that now. But when you know. When you see what I've been hiding—"

He didn't press her further. Not this time. Instead, Thomas let the silence stretch between them, the weight of their unspoken truths pressing heavy in the air.

Finally, he reached for her hand. Just a whisper of contact, his fingers brushing hers.

"I'm not leaving, Constantine. I'm not asking for answers tonight. I'm just asking you not to shut me out."

The sincerity in his voice broke something loose inside her.

For the first time since discovering the truth, she felt the tiniest crack in her carefully constructed armor.

Her voice, fragile but honest, was barely audible. "I'm trying, Thomas. I am. But I don't know how to stop being afraid."

He nodded slowly, stepping back just enough to give her space while holding her gaze. "When you're ready...I'll be here. No matter what."

A silence fell between them, but it wasn't cold or distant. It was fragile. Tender.

Abigail's voice broke the quiet from across the hall, "I'll lock up. You two go on ahead."

Constantine turned to Abigail, then back to Thomas, drawing a shaky breath as she forced herself to meet his gaze one last time.

"Thank you," she whispered.

He gave a small nod, a promise that didn't need words.

And for the first time, as they stepped out into the late afternoon air, Constantine felt the weight of her secret begin to shift.

Because even if the truth would one day break them. He wasn't leaving yet. And for now, that was enough.

35

The sun had dipped low, casting a warm amber glow over Puckerbrush. The scent of lilacs lingered on Constantine's sweater, subtle yet sweet, as she stood near the steps of the community center, watching the last of the guests disappear down the quiet main street.

Thomas hadn't left either. He stood just a few feet away, hands in his pockets, his expression thoughtful as he looked out over the street, the hush between them broken only by the faint melody of wind chimes echoing from the porch.

It would have been easier to leave. To slip away before the quiet stretched into something too intimate, too vulnerable. But he stayed. And so did she.

At last, his voice cut through the silence, low and steady. "I'm heading over to the café. Want to come? Just coffee."

The day had been long, and she hesitated. The baby shower was filled with so much laughter and warmth, but the weight pressing against her chest remained. And yet, there was something steady about the way he stood there, not demanding anything, just offering.

She exhaled slowly. "Yeah. That sounds nice."

The Puckerbrush Café felt unchanged. The scent of coffee

lingered warm and familiar in the air, mingling with the sweetness of pastries cooling behind the glass display case where Emily was carefully labeling slices of apple pie.

John stood at the counter, wiping down a row of mugs with his usual quiet focus, but when his gaze met Constantine's, there was a subtle softness in his expression.

"Evening, you two," Emily called, her voice light but sharp enough to make Constantine blush.

She mustered a smile. "Hey, Emily."

John asked, "What can we get you two?"

Thomas looked to Constantine, giving her the space to decline, but she nodded gently. "Coffee, please."

Without another word, John set about gathering two mugs and a fresh pot of coffee while Constantine sank into the corner booth by the window. Outside, the streetlamps flickered to life against the purple sky, the hum of the ceiling fan the only sound filling the quiet space.

Thomas slid into the seat across from her, leaning back slightly as if waiting for her to settle before speaking. John placed the mugs on the table and filled them both.

"Long day?" Thomas asked gently after John returned to the counter.

She huffed a quiet laugh, wrapping her hands around the warm mug in front of her. "You could say that. I've officially reached my limit on pastel tissue paper and baby shower games."

Thomas smirked. "I'll keep that in mind for next time."

The teasing eased some of the tension from her chest, but the quiet stretched again. Not uncomfortable but weighted. Something unspoken pressed between them, just beneath the surface.

After a beat, he broke the silence.

"So...we're here. No shower chaos. No town history lectures. Just coffee." His voice was softer but still laced with a quiet sincerity. "Feels like a good time to ask random questions."

She blinked, surprised. "Random questions?"

He nodded, leaning forward with his elbows resting lightly on the worn tabletop. "Yeah. You know, to get out of our own heads for a minute. I'll go first."

The corner of her mouth lifted in a small, reluctant smile. "Alright."

Thomas's gaze softened, his voice gentle. "What's something you've always wanted to do but never had the chance?"

The question caught her off guard. She'd expected something easier, like her favorite book or if she preferred the beach or the mountains. But he wasn't giving her the easy way out.

Constantine hesitated, fingers tracing the rim of her mug as she thought.

"Travel," she admitted finally, her voice quieter now. "I've always wanted to really travel. Not just for work or to see family, but somewhere far, somewhere that didn't feel familiar. Maybe Italy. Or Greece. I like the idea of getting lost in a place where no one knows my name. No expectations. Just...being."

Thomas nodded, his gaze steady and warm as he listened. "That sounds incredible. You should do it someday."

She offered a faint smile. "Maybe." But even as she said it, a part of her felt the weight pressing back in, because how could she think about her dreams when she was holding so much back?

She cleared her throat and tilted her head toward him. "Your turn. What's something you always wanted to do?"

His smile lingered, but it shifted into something quieter. "I've always wanted to learn how to play guitar. Never got around to it, but it's still on the list."

Her eyebrows lifted, genuinely surprised. "You? Musical?"

He chuckled. "Said I wanted to. Never said I was good at it."

Their laughter mingled with the soft clink of mugs on the table, the vulnerability easing, but not disappearing. Something deeper still lingered beneath their words, the tension neither of them had fully named.

Thomas's expression shifted more seriously as his gaze held hers. "You know, I really liked today. Not just the baby shower. This." He gestured between them. "Being around you. When you're not holding back so much."

The words landed softly, but the weight pressed harder, because he was right. She was holding back. Not because she didn't want to be close. But because telling him the truth could change everything. And she wasn't ready for that. Not yet.

So, instead, she offered a quiet smile, lowering her gaze as her fingers curled more tightly around the warmth of her mug.

"Me too," she whispered.

For now, it was all she could give. And for now, it was enough.

36

Pale gray light struggled to break through the morning mist lingering over the fields as rain tapped softly against the motel windows. The scent of damp earth clung to the air, the storm from the night before leaving everything hushed and still.

Constantine sat on the edge of her bed, a half-empty cup of tea cooling in her hands, her gaze fixed on the rain-streaked glass.

She had slept little. Not with Thomas's words still echoing in her mind, *When you're not holding back so much.*

He hadn't meant to push her last night at the café. If anything, he'd been patient, almost too patient, offering quiet space instead of demands, kindness instead of pressure. And somehow, that made it harder. Because it wasn't trust that kept her silent. It was the truth itself.

Her stomach twisted as the familiar ache settled back into her chest.

She should have told him by now. Should have found the words to explain why she'd kept him at arm's length, why she'd held back the truth about Eldon and Edward Dalton.

But how do you tell someone you care about that your family's past is tangled up with the death of his great-grandfather?

A soft knock at the door startled her from her thoughts.

Constantine hesitated before setting her cup down and crossing the room. Through the window, she caught a glimpse of Thomas's familiar figure standing just outside.

His hair was damp from the rain, his sleeves rolled up slightly as he held a brown paper bag in one hand and two steaming cups of coffee in the other.

When she opened the door, his smile was small but genuine. "Morning."

"Morning." Her voice felt too quiet.

He shifted, holding up the bag as if to explain himself. "Brought coffee. And muffins. Emily insisted."

Her lips curved. "She would."

The drizzle outside had dampened his shirt collar, the mist making his hair curl slightly at the edges. He looked tired. As if he'd been thinking as much as she had since last night.

She stepped back without a word, letting him inside.

The room felt even smaller with him there, the rain-softened light casting pale shadows along the worn floral bedspread and the simple wooden desk tucked near the window. But Thomas didn't seem to notice. He set the coffees and the bag on the desk, then turned to face her.

"I figured we could keep the small-talk-only thing going," he said.

She nodded, pressing her hands together to still the trembling. "Thanks for the coffee."

Silence lingered between them, heavier than before. The rain blurred the world outside, wrapping the motel in a gray stillness that seemed to press more closely around them.

She knew he wasn't here just for muffins. And he wasn't leaving.

Thomas exhaled quietly, watching her in that same patient way he had last night as if he could sense the words she wasn't saying. Finally, he spoke, "Constantine...I know there's more going on. I'm not asking for everything. But I'm not blind, either."

Her heart twisted, the guilt pressing harder. "I'm not trying to hurt you," she whispered, voice breaking slightly.

"I know." His voice stayed calm, steady. "But you're keeping something back. And I'm just—" He ran a hand through his damp hair, exhaling. "I care about you. I'm not here for the history or the old family secrets. I'm here for you. But I can't keep feeling like you're afraid to let me in."

The words struck harder than she expected, unraveling something she had been holding together for too long. She swallowed hard, arms crossing over her chest to shield herself from the weight pressing in.

"I'm not afraid of you," she said. "I'm afraid of what the truth could do. To us. To everything we've—"

Her voice caught, breaking off before she could finish.

Thomas nodded slowly, stepping closer but careful not to reach for her.

"Whatever it is," he said, his voice rough with sincerity, "I'm still here. I just need you to trust me enough to tell me. Because keeping this between us hurts more than the truth ever could."

Constantine blinked hard, fighting the burn behind her eyes.

But what if the truth is worse?

What if telling him about Eldon and Edward Dalton changed everything? Not just how he saw her, but how he saw his own family?

"I don't know if I can," she whispered.

A flicker of frustration crossed his face for the first time, but it softened almost instantly, replaced by something gentler.

"Then let me stay anyway." His voice was quieter now, almost a plea. "Don't shut me out. Whatever this is...we'll face it together. If you let me."

The ache swelled, fierce and overwhelming, but beneath it was something warmer. A thread of hope she hadn't let herself feel in too long. Maybe he wouldn't leave. Maybe he meant it. And yet, the words still wouldn't come.

So instead, she nodded, forcing a shaky breath as she whispered, "Okay."

Thomas held her gaze a moment longer, searching her face for something she wasn't sure how to give. Then, quietly, he nodded, too.

For now, it was enough.

But she knew, eventually, she'd have to give him the truth he deserved.

37

The rain lifted by noon, leaving behind a damp stillness that clung to the air as the clouds thinned and pale streaks of sunlight broke through the gray. The fields beyond the Puckerbrush Motel were hazy, damp mist rising from the soil in soft ribbons as if the earth itself was exhaling after the storm.

Constantine sat on the low stone bench just beyond the motel parking lot, her tea long since gone cold in the paper cup resting beside her. She barely noticed the chill, her gaze lost in the horizon as the faint scent of rain-soaked lilacs drifted on the breeze.

She wasn't sure how long she'd been sitting there, only that the silence felt heavier with every passing moment, her thoughts circling back to the same knot of emotions that had weighed on her since morning. Thomas had left her room with no anger, no frustration, just patience and the quiet reassurance that he wasn't going anywhere.

She wanted to believe that. But the ache lingered, sharper now that the words she couldn't bring herself to say pressed tightly against her ribs.

The sound of footsteps drew her from her thoughts, steady and familiar, and even before she turned, she knew who it was. Thomas.

He slowed as he approached, hands tucked loosely into the pockets of his jacket, his expression uncertain but determined, as if he had spent as much time thinking as she had.

"I saw you out here," he said, his voice low but steady, as though explaining his presence. "Figured I'd check in."

Glancing up at him, she forced a small smile that felt fragile at the edges. "I'm fine."

Thomas didn't look convinced but didn't press. Instead, he settled onto the other end of the bench, leaving just enough space between them to keep the moment from feeling too heavy, though his presence was more grounding than she expected.

Neither spoke for a long while, quiet stretching between them as the wind stirred the scent of wildflowers and damp grass.

Finally, Thomas broke the silence, his voice soft but sure. "You don't have to keep saying you're fine when you're not."

The words settled between them, gentle but weighted, and Constantine felt her pulse quicken despite the calm in his tone. She exhaled slowly, her fingers knotting together in her lap as she spoke, her voice barely above a whisper, "I'm not trying to shut you out. I just...I don't know how to explain all this without making things worse."

Thomas didn't press further, didn't fill the silence with questions or expectations. He just waited, his quiet patience creating a space for her to speak if she chose to, and that made it harder somehow, the sincerity in his gaze unraveling the walls she had worked so hard to keep in place.

"I'm scared," she admitted finally, her voice breaking slightly. "Not of you. But of what happens when you know the truth? Because once I say it...once it's out there, I can't take it back."

She glanced at him, expecting to find confusion or doubt, but there was neither. Instead, he nodded slowly, his brow furrowing as he shifted slightly to face her.

"Constantine, I'm not asking you to rush this. And I'm not here for perfect answers. I just need you to trust me enough to know that whatever it is, it won't change how I feel about you."

Her breath caught, the sincerity in his words pressing deeper than she expected, loosening the knot twisted even as it made her throat tighten.

"I don't know how you can say that," she whispered, her voice trembling. "How can you make that promise without knowing what I'm keeping from you?"

Thomas hesitated, exhaling as he leaned forward slightly, resting his forearms on his knees, his gaze steady.

"Because I know you. And that's enough for me."

Neither spoke for a long moment.

And then Thomas shifted, his tone quieter now, almost tentative. "There's a lot I don't know about you yet. And I don't want to push you into anything you're not ready for. But if you're willing..." He paused, glancing at her as if searching for the right words. "Would you have dinner with me tonight? Just the two of us. No pressure. Just time to talk. Or not talk if that's what you need."

Constantine blinked, the unexpectedness of the invitation catching her off guard. "Dinner?"

Thomas nodded, his expression softening just slightly.

"Yeah. Dinner. Somewhere quiet. But if you feel you can't, if you don't think you're ready to let me in, then I'll leave tomorrow morning and give you the space you need. It won't change how I feel, but I don't want to make this harder for you."

Her chest tightened at his words, the quiet sincerity in his voice cutting through her defenses in a way she wasn't prepared for. He wasn't threatening to leave. He wasn't giving her an ultimatum. He was giving her a choice. That made it harder somehow because she didn't want him to go.

"I'll think about it," she breathed, her voice breaking slightly around the words.

Thomas nodded once, rising slowly from the bench but not stepping away immediately. He stood there, his hand brushing lightly against the back of the bench as if he wanted to say more but chose not to.

"I'll be around," he mumbled, his gaze meeting hers one last time before he turned toward the motel, his footsteps soft against the damp grass.

Watching him go, the angst shifted slightly, just enough to let in something warmer.

She wasn't ready yet. But maybe, just maybe, she was closer than she thought.

Constantine stayed on the bench long after Thomas walked away, her tea still untouched beside her, the paper cup damp with condensation. She watched him retreat toward his motel room, his steps slow but purposeful, the sound of his boots fading into the damp stillness of the afternoon.

He hadn't pressed her. Even as he offered her dinner, he offered her time and space to talk or simply be. He had given her a choice.

And for the first time in longer than she could remember, the angst she carried felt less like a burden she had to carry alone and more like a bridge waiting to be crossed.

By the time she stood, the clouds had thinned further, streaks of pale sunlight breaking through to warm the damp earth. The air smelled clean, fresh, as if the storm had taken more than just the rain with it. By the time she reached her room, she'd made her decision.

Setting the tea down on the small desk, Constantine paused, her gaze lingering on the closed door. The thought of calling Thomas felt wrong, too impersonal. She wanted to say it to his face.

She didn't let herself hesitate. Stepping out into the parking lot, she walked the short distance to his room, her heart quickening as she raised her hand to knock.

The door opened a few moments later, and there he was. His hair slightly mussed, sleeves pushed up casually as if he'd been lost in his own thoughts. His brow lifted slightly when he saw her, but the lingering concern in his expression softened almost instantly.

"Constantine," he breathed, his voice careful but warm. "Everything okay?"

She nodded, though her chest still felt tight, her hands brushing absently against the fabric of her sweater.

"I didn't want to leave this hanging," she began softly, her voice steadier than she expected. "I've got plans with Abigail and the kids this afternoon, but if dinner is still on the table, I can be ready by seven."

Thomas simply looked at her, the faintest flicker of surprise crossing his features before his mouth curved into a small, genuine smile.

"It's definitely still on the table," he said, his voice soft but sure.

Constantine's shoulders eased, the tension she hadn't realized she was holding, releasing slightly at his response.

"Okay," she said, her lips lifting into a tentative smile. "Seven, then."

Thomas nodded, his gaze steady on hers. "Seven. I'll pick you up."

She hesitated, feeling the moment settle between them, but his expression remained so open, so patient, that it steadied her even as her heart fluttered.

"I'll see you then," she murmured.

And as she turned to go, her steps lighter than they had been all day, Constantine realized that maybe, just maybe, the dinner wasn't about finding the perfect words or answers. Maybe it was just about showing up.

38

The rain returned by dusk, curling in a fine mist along the window edges and softening the view of the fields beyond the motel into pale gray smudges. The world outside seemed muted, but inside Constantine's room, the air felt heavier, the storm pressing against her ribs as the truth she had carried for so long threatened to spill out.

Dinner had been simple, comfortable, and yet something about the evening had shifted her perspective.

Thomas had taken her to the Puckerbrush Café, the small but beloved heart of the town, filled with the scent of roasted coffee and fresh pie. They had chosen a corner booth by the window, the rain streaking faint patterns against the glass as they talked about everything but the weight between them. Childhood stories, the quirks of an author's life, even a few dry jokes about the stubborn weather.

For the first time, the silence between them didn't feel heavy. Stepping into her room, the warmth of the café still lingering on her skin, the ache inside her shifted. The truth, heavy as it was, had waited long enough.

Thomas shrugged off his jacket, draping it neatly over the back of the chair by the desk, his movements calm, unhurried. His steady presence grounded her as he turned back to face her, his brow lifting slightly in question.

"You okay?" he asked gently, his voice careful but not hesitant.

Standing by the window, her arms wrapped lightly around herself as she watched the faint trails of mist curling along the glass, her reflection stared back at her, faint and fragile, but she didn't let herself turn away this time.

"No," she said, her voice trembling just slightly. "Not yet."

Thomas's expression softened, the concern in his gaze deepening as he crossed the room, stopping just short of where she stood as if giving her space to decide what came next.

"Talk to me," he whispered, his steadiness offering her an opening without pushing.

Her fingers tightened against her arms, her breath catching as she forced herself to speak.

"Thomas, what I need to tell you is something I've been carrying for a long time. And I'm scared. Scared that once I tell you, once you know, you'll leave."

His brow furrowed, but he didn't move, his patience unwavering.

"I'm listening," he said.

Her throat tightened, the words pressing painfully against her chest, but she pushed through, her voice breaking slightly as she began. "It's about Edward Dalton. About what happened to him. And my family."

The name lingered in the air between them, heavy and raw, but Thomas didn't flinch.

"My great-great-uncle Eldon," she continued, her words faltering but determined, "he... he killed your great-grandfather."

The silence that followed was sharp, echoing louder than the rain against the window, but Constantine forced herself to keep going, her voice trembling with the weight of what she needed him to understand.

"Edward Dalton came to Puckerbrush during one of his revivals," she said, her hands clenching tightly at her sides. "He wasn't just preaching, Thomas. He took advantage of people. Of their faith, their trust. He hurt them, including my great-great-uncle's daughter, Mary. She was just a girl. She believed him. She trusted him."

Her breath hitched, tears stinging at the edges of her vision, but she pressed on.

"When she became pregnant, he left. He disappeared and left her to face it alone. And Mary..." Her voice cracked. "She died giving birth. Eldon had already lost his wife the same way. Losing his daughter...it broke him. Completely."

Thomas's expression remained still, his jaw tight, but the raw and unguarded emotion in his eyes made her falter.

"And when Dalton came back for another revival, Eldon confronted him. He wanted answers, but Dalton denied everything."

The words were sharp and raw, but they spilled out before she could stop them.

"Eldon killed him," she whispered. "And he didn't just kill him, Thomas. He buried him in a field somewhere, took the money from the revival, and left Mary's baby, his grandchild, at the baby hatch at the orphanage. He thought it was the only way to give the child a chance at something better. And he never spoke about it again until he confessed to Abigail on his deathbed."

Her voice broke completely, her chest tightening as she looked away, unable to meet Thomas's gaze any longer.

"I didn't know how to tell you," she whispered, her hands trembling at her sides. "I thought...I thought it would ruin everything. That you'd see me differently. That you'd leave."

Rain tapping softly against the window was the only sound for a long moment.

Then, slowly, carefully, Thomas moved, closing the distance between them, raising his hand to cup her face with a gentleness that sent fresh tears slipping down her cheeks.

"Look at me," he whispered, his voice low but firm.

Her breath caught, but she forced herself to meet his gaze, her heart pounding as the silence stretched between them.

"You thought I'd blame you?" he asked, his voice trembling just slightly.

She nodded, unable to speak.

Thomas shook his head, his thumb brushing away a tear as he leaned in to rest his brow gently against hers.

"This is...it's a lot," he admitted, his voice rough but steady. "But none of this is your fault, Constantine. You didn't do this. You didn't make those choices. And it doesn't change how I feel about you."

Her breath hitched, fresh tears slipping free as she gripped his hands tightly.

"But it feels like it does," she whispered. "It feels like I've been carrying it forever, and I didn't know how to let you in without losing you."

His voice softened further. His grip was steady as he pulled her closer.

"You're not losing me," he murmured. "I'm still here. I'm not going anywhere."

And as his arms wrapped fully around her, the pain that had pressed so heavily against her chest eased.

For the first time, the weight of the past felt lighter.

For the first time, she let herself believe maybe she hadn't lost everything after all.

39

The rain quieted to a gentle hush outside, the mist softening as twilight deepened into night. The fields beyond the window were barely visible now, cloaked in pale gray shadows, but neither Constantine nor Thomas noticed.

They faced each other in the quiet, the angst between them slowly dissolving into something softer. Something unspoken.

Thomas's hands cradled hers, his grip steady but light, as though he was giving her the space to pull away if she needed it. But she didn't want to. Not tonight.

The truth was finally out, raw, painful, but no longer hers alone to bear.

And yet, there was still so much more.

She looked up at him, the tension in her chest lingering not from fear anymore but from the sheer weight of his tenderness, the way he saw her, even now, without judgment.

"I don't know how to let this go," she whispered, voice fragile but honest.

His thumb traced gently over the back of her hand, a simple, grounding gesture that sent warmth spreading through her.

"You don't have to let it go," he said. "You're allowed to feel this,

Constantine. You're allowed to grieve for what happened. But you don't have to carry it alone anymore."

The words pressed deeper than she expected, unraveling something even more fragile inside her. She felt the sting of tears returning, but this time, they weren't sharp with guilt. They were something else. Something closer to release.

Her breath hitched as she stepped closer, pressing her forehead against his chest, the warmth of him steadying her in ways she hadn't thought possible.

Thomas exhaled a shaky breath against her hair, his arms wrapping carefully around her as though holding her together without asking for anything more.

But she wanted more. She had never felt so close to him, not just physically, but in the quiet way he had stayed when she had given him every reason to leave.

"Thomas," she whispered, tilting her head just enough to meet his gaze again.

His eyes darkened, searching hers as though asking for permission, his breath catching slightly when she lifted her hand to his face, fingers trailing along the edge of his jaw.

And then, carefully, she closed the space between them.

The kiss was soft at first. A hesitant whisper of contact more than anything else. But the way Thomas responded, the way his hand slid gently along the curve of her waist, the quiet exhale he gave as he deepened the kiss, made her feel safe. Anchored.

It wasn't rushed. It wasn't desperate. It was right.

When they finally pulled back, the room felt warmer, the tension replaced with something quieter, more certain. His forehead rested against hers, their breaths mingling.

"I'm still here," he whispered. "I'm not leaving."

This time, Constantine believed him. She reached for him again, the pain shifting into something more. Something she was finally ready to share.

When their lips met this time, it wasn't just comfort they found. It was healing.

The rain slowed to nothing more than a soft whisper against the windows, the mist blurring the edges of the world beyond the glass. The room felt warmer somehow, though neither Constantine nor Thomas had moved from where they stood. They were still close, still holding on in the quiet aftermath of her confession.

The truth was out. Raw. Unforgiving. But it no longer sat like a weight pressing against her chest.

He was still here. Thomas hadn't turned away, hadn't recoiled. And that truth, more than anything else, left her feeling both exposed and safe.

The air between them felt different now, charged with something softer, quieter, yet undeniable.

His hands still held hers, steady despite the emotion she could feel vibrating just beneath his skin, the tension in his shoulders slowly easing. She could feel the strength in his grip, the way his thumb brushed absently across her knuckles as if reminding her— *I'm not leaving. I'm still here.*

She had been so certain he would leave. But he hadn't. And something inside her broke open at the realization.

Her voice was barely more than a whisper. "I don't know how to let this go, Thomas. I don't know how to stop carrying it."

His brow furrowed, and without hesitation, he reached up, gently tucking a strand of hair behind her ear, the tenderness in his touch unraveling her defenses even further.

"You don't have to let it go," he said. "You just have to stop carrying it alone."

Her breath caught on the words, a tremor working its way through her as his hand lingered at the curve of her face, warm and solid. She hadn't realized how much she had been longing for that. Just to be held, not out of comfort, but out of understanding.

And then she moved closer, her forehead pressing gently to his chest, her fingers curling against the fabric of his shirt as the pain growing inside gave way to something else, something quieter.

Relief. Grief. Hope.

Thomas exhaled slowly, wrapping his arms around her and

holding her as if she might break, but trusting her strength all the same. His heartbeat was steady beneath her cheek, grounding her in a way she wasn't familiar with.

They stayed like that for a long moment, the quiet pressing in, the rain beyond the window nothing more than a gentle hush.

But it wasn't enough. Not anymore.

She lifted her head, heart pounding for a very different reason as her gaze met his, so steady, so present.

"Thomas." Her voice trembled slightly, but her hand rose, fingertips tracing the line of his jaw, feeling the warmth of his skin beneath her touch.

His eyes darkened, searching hers, breath catching as though waiting for permission.

Softly, she gave it.

She leaned in first, brushing her lips against his with a softness so fragile she felt her heart stutter.

The kiss was hesitant, almost questioning, until he responded, his hand cupping her face more fully, thumb tracing along her cheek as he deepened it just slightly, his breath warm against her skin.

It wasn't rushed. It wasn't desperate. It was everything she hadn't known she needed. This quiet, undeniable pull between them layered with all the words they couldn't quite say yet.

When they parted, she kept her eyes closed, her forehead resting lightly against his, their breath mingling as she tried to gather herself.

But there was no going back from this. And she didn't want to.

When she finally opened her eyes, she found him watching her as if memorizing every detail, like he was still waiting for her to decide.

"I don't want to be afraid anymore," she whispered, her voice breaking slightly. "Not with you."

Something shifted in his expression, became softer but no less intense.

"You don't have to be."

And he kissed her again, deeper this time, his hand sliding gently from her face to her waist, drawing her closer in a way that felt both protective and unyielding.

The heat between them built slowly, cautiously, like the fear lingering between them had finally found release.

Her hands fisted in the fabric of his shirt, pulling him closer until there was no space left between them, until she felt the solid press of his chest against hers, the quiet strength in the way he held her. She felt safe.

When his lips moved along the curve of her jaw, pressing gentle kisses there, she whispered his name again, softer this time, the sound breaking between them.

"Tell me if you want me to stop," he murmured, his voice low, breath warm against her skin.

She shook her head, her fingers curling more tightly at his back. "Don't stop."

And he didn't.

They moved together with a tenderness she hadn't known she was capable of. Every touch, every kiss speaking more than words could. There was no urgency, no rush to claim or take. Only a steady, unspoken promise in the way he laid her back on the bed, his hand tracing reverent paths along her skin as if to remind her: *You are safe. You are wanted. You are enough.*

The walls she had built so carefully, the ones she had clung to out of fear and guilt, had already crumbled.

And when she whispered his name again, pressing her lips to his, she knew. They were gone completely.

40

The rain stopped during the night, leaving the air heavy with the scent of damp earth and lilacs as dawn crept gently through the cracks in the curtains. Pale light painted soft patterns along the walls, casting everything in muted gold.

Constantine lay still, her head resting against Thomas's chest, the steady rhythm of his heartbeat beneath her ear as constant as the warmth of his arm wrapped loosely around her waist. His breath came slow and even, his body relaxed in sleep, but she couldn't quiet the thoughts circling in her mind.

For the first time in longer than she could remember, the ache she had carried so fiercely, the guilt, the fear of losing him, had eased. Thomas was still here.

He had listened to her. He had held her as she confessed everything, his steady presence anchoring her when the weight of the truth threatened to pull her under. And yet, even as calm settled over her, there was a part of her that felt exposed, vulnerable in a way she wasn't prepared for.

She shifted slightly, careful not to disturb him, but Thomas stirred anyway, a soft exhale escaping as his arm tightened gently around her, his lips brushing the top of her head.

"Hey," he murmured, voice thick with sleep, rough and quiet.

Constantine froze for a heartbeat, her pulse quickening as his fingers traced slow, lazy circles along her back.

"I didn't mean to wake you," she whispered.

He hummed softly, pressing another kiss to her hair. "I don't mind."

They fell silent again, the morning hush wrapping around them like a blanket, but this time, the quiet felt lighter. Easier.

After a while, Thomas shifted, pulling back just enough to meet her gaze, his eyes still heavy-lidded but warm. He brushed his thumb gently along her cheek, his brow furrowing slightly as he searched her face.

"You okay?" he asked, his voice tender, but there was a quiet certainty beneath the words, as though he already knew she wasn't.

Constantine hesitated, her fingers brushing absently against the warmth of his chest. "I keep waiting for it to feel...different," she admitted softly. "I thought telling you everything would make it all go away. And it did, in a way. But it still feels heavy."

Thomas didn't speak right away, letting her words settle between them. His gaze never wavered as he rolled onto his side, his hand moving to cradle her face with the same steady tenderness that had undone her the night before.

"This," he said, his voice was quiet but certain, "this wasn't just comfort, Constantine. It wasn't temporary. You trusted me. And I meant what I said last night that I'm not leaving."

Her breath caught, tears stinging the edges of her eyes.

"What happened with our families," he continued, his firm voice edged with sadness, "is awful. And it hurts. But it doesn't change what I feel for you. It never could."

The ache shifted, breaking into something warmer, something fragile but no longer unbearable.

"But what if it's too much?" she whispered, her voice trembling. "What if the distance? Our lives? It's just too hard?"

"It's not," he replied, pressing his brow gently to hers. "It's not too much. Not for us."

She closed her eyes, his words settling deep, but the fear still lingered at the edges of her mind, the uncertainty of what came next pressing harder against her ribs.

"I don't want to lose you," she whispered, her voice cracking now. "I don't want this to be something we look back on someday, wishing we'd tried harder."

Thomas shook his head before she could finish, his grip on her hand tightening as he leaned closer.

"You're not going to lose me," he murmured roughly. "I *chose* you, Constantine. I *choose* you now, and I'll keep choosing you, no matter how hard it gets. But we have to figure out what that looks like. Together."

Tears slipped down her cheeks, and she blinked hard, her fingers curling tightly against his chest.

"How?" she whispered, the doubt pressing harder even as his words filled her with hope.

Thomas smiled faintly, brushing a tear from her cheek with his thumb.

"We talk. We figure it out one step at a time. My life is in Fairview, my work, my family, but that doesn't mean I can't be with you too. It doesn't mean we can't make this work. I want this, Constantine. I want you."

Her breath hitched at the quiet certainty in his voice, the way he spoke as though his words were undeniable.

"I want you too," she said, her voice breaking as she leaned into him fully, the last of her walls crumbling as his arms closed around her again. "I don't know how we'll do it, but I want this, Thomas."

His lips found hers then, the kiss slow and lingering. Not a question but an answer, a promise sealed between them in the quiet hush of the morning.

As Constantine held him tighter, felt the warmth of his presence grounding her completely, she realized that perhaps the ache she had feared, the ache of distance, wasn't the same thing as loss.

Maybe, just maybe, it was a reminder. That what they had was real. And worth holding on to.

41

Wood smoke lingered in Abigail and Matthew's farmhouse, mingling with the aroma of steeped chamomile and fresh bread cooling on the kitchen counter. The fire crackled softly in the hearth, filling the space with a gentle warmth that contrasted the gray drizzle clinging stubbornly to the fields beyond the rain-streaked windows.

It felt safe here. Familiar. And yet, the quiet tension that had settled between them was undeniable.

Constantine sat close to Thomas at the worn oak table, her fingers curling around the stoneware mug Abigail had placed in front of her, though the tea had long since cooled. Their knees brushing beneath the table, Thomas's presence was steady as he waited for her to speak.

Across from them, Abigail sat with her hands folded gently on the table, the familiar lines of her face softened with concern as she watched them both, sensing without knowing that something unspoken was hanging in the air.

Matthew lingered near the window, arms crossed loosely over his chest, gaze fixed on the pale mist curling along the edges of the pasture. He hadn't spoken yet, but Constantine could feel his attention, the quiet weight of his protective nature, as though he was bracing for whatever was coming.

She hadn't realized how hard this would be. But she had made her choice.

Clearing her throat, Constantine set the untouched mug aside and lifted her gaze, forcing herself to meet Abigail's eyes directly.

"I told him." Her voice was quieter than she intended but steady. "About Eldon. About Edward Dalton. Everything."

For a heartbeat, there was only the crackle of the fire and the faint patter of rain against the windows.

Abigail's breath caught, though she quickly pressed her lips together, her eyes flicking toward Thomas as if searching his face for some sign of anger or heartbreak.

Steady as ever, Thomas spoke before the silence could press too heavily.

"I needed to know," he said, his voice calm but weighted with emotion. "And I understand now why you kept it from me. I understand why you both felt it was better not to tell my family. It wasn't about protecting a lie. It was about sparing them a truth they didn't need."

Abigail exhaled softly, nodding as her gaze returned to Constantine, her expression searching. "And you both agree that keeping the secret is what you want?"

Constantine swallowed, reaching for Thomas's hand beneath the table, feeling the solid warmth of his fingers closing gently around hers.

"We've decided not to tell anyone else," she whispered. "We believe...his family has made peace with the belief that Edward Dalton disappeared. Bringing this back into the light won't change anything for the better. It will only cause pain for people who don't deserve to carry it."

Abigail's gaze softened, but Matthew spoke first, his voice low and measured as he turned back from the window, "You're sure about this?"

Thomas nodded, the certainty in his voice unwavering.

"I am." His eyes remained steady on Matthew's, calm but unyielding. "I've thought about this. I don't need answers about my great-grandfather's past. I don't need to trace every step back to understand who he was or what he did. What matters now, what always mattered, is the life I'm building here. With Constantine. And I won't let the past steal that from us."

Matthew's expression shifted, the lines on his face easing, though the protective set of his shoulders never quite relaxed. After a beat, he nodded.

"I think you're doing the right thing," he said. "That story...it's heavy. But it doesn't have to define either of you."

Abigail pressed a hand gently to her chest, nodding slowly. "I kept Eldon's journals for so long because I thought...maybe he was asking to be remembered. To be forgiven. But you're right. Sometimes the most loving thing we can do is choose to let a story end."

"And Dr. Harper?" Matthew asked. "Do you think she'll let the story end?"

Constantine looked at Thomas. It wasn't a question she could answer.

"I believe so," Thomas replied with a firm nod. "I believe that she understands dredging up the past doesn't always make things better. It prolongs the pain."

He and Matthew shared a look, and the tension in Matthew's shoulders seemed to lessen.

Constantine felt her chest tighten, not with sadness but with the quiet feeling of release, of knowing they were not alone in this choice.

And yet, there was still more.

"We're leaving soon," she added softly, glancing toward Thomas. "I wanted you both to know before we left town. To hear it directly from us. We won't forget what happened here. But we're choosing to move forward."

Thomas nodded, his hand squeezing hers gently as if to echo the promise.

They would leave Puckerbrush soon. The past would stay behind. And their future, their story, would belong only to them.

Eyes glistening, Abigail reached across the table, her hand covering Constantine's with a tenderness so familiar it made her throat tighten.

"I'm proud of you," she whispered, voice breaking just slightly. "Both of you. Not because you're leaving, but because you've chosen each other. Because you've chosen to let go of a burden that was never yours to carry."

Matthew nodded once, a quiet approval in his gaze as he looked toward Thomas.

"You take care of each other," he added, his voice softer than before. "That's what matters."

And as Constantine met Thomas's gaze once more, seeing not just reassurance but love, steadfast and certain, she knew they would.

Together.

42

T hey stood in the parking lot of the Puckerbrush Motel, the rain-slicked pavement shimmering beneath the pale gold light of late morning, the mist having lifted entirely. Behind them, the town stretched out, familiar landmarks softened by the distance. The steeple of the small church, the narrow streets lined with weathered buildings, and the green fields stretching endlessly toward the horizon.

Constantine stood beside her car, her fingers brushing the keys in her palm, feeling the weight of the moment settle over her.

She had imagined leaving Puckerbrush would be difficult, that it would feel like closing the door on something unfinished. But as she glanced toward Thomas, who stood only a few steps away, leaning against the hood of his car, she realized the ache she had feared wasn't as sharp as she'd expected. It felt right.

Puckerbrush had been tied to the burdens of her family's past for so long, but now, the town felt different. It wasn't just the place where she'd uncovered long-buried secrets. It was a place where she had been welcomed, where she had healed.

Thomas studied her, then offered a small, knowing smile. "You okay?"

She let out a breath, nodding. "I think so. It's strange, but I don't feel like I'm leaving anything behind. I feel like I'm taking it with me."

His expression softened, and he reached out, brushing his fingers over hers before she turned her hand to lace them together.

"You are," he murmured. "Puckerbrush will always be a part of you. Of us."

Her chest tightened, but this time, it wasn't from sadness. It was gratitude. She thought of Abigail and Matthew, their steady warmth and quiet wisdom. Piper's kindness and Lydia's steady nature. Emily's sharp humor and John's constant presence beside her at the café. The gentle reassurance of Martha and Charles.

She thought of bright, boisterous Berta, who had made her laugh on days when she thought she couldn't.

"I want to take them with me," Constantine admitted, her voice thick with emotion. "I don't want to forget how they welcomed me when I showed up here, how they became family when I didn't even know I needed one." She swallowed hard. "I don't know where I'll end up, but I want them with me, somehow."

Thomas squeezed her hand. "You won't forget them. They're part of you now. Wherever we go, they'll come with us."

She nodded, blinking back tears, then let out a soft laugh. "So, I guess this is it."

Thomas exhaled, glancing around the quiet parking lot before meeting her gaze again. "For now."

They stood for a moment longer, neither quite ready to move, until finally Constantine took a steadying breath and turned toward her car.

Thomas did the same, opening the driver's side door, then pausing with his hand on the frame.

"I'll follow you," he said, his voice gentle but firm. "At least until we hit the main highway."

Constantine smiled, warmth filling her chest. "I'd like that."

With one last glance at each other, they got into their cars.

Constantine pulled out of the parking lot, glancing in her

rearview mirror and seeing Thomas just behind her, his headlights steady, unwavering.

As they passed the wooden *Welcome to Puckerbrush* sign at the edge of town, its cheerful *Come Back Soon!* painted in bright, fading letters, she let out a soft breath she hadn't realized she was holding.

"Do you think we'll come back someday?" she asked aloud, more to herself than anyone else.

Thomas's voice crackled softly over the speakerphone in her car.

"Maybe," he said thoughtfully. "But only if you want to. Our story isn't here anymore, Constantine. It's wherever we decide to go next."

Her heart swelled at the quiet certainty of his words.

She looked ahead at the road stretching before her, wide and open, wildflowers beaded with rain on either side.

"What's next?" she asked, her voice catching slightly on the question.

There was a pause, then the warmth of his voice filled the car again.

"Whatever we want."

And for the first time, the thought of what came next didn't scare her. It thrilled her.

She let the sun-warmed breeze wash over her through the open window, and as Puckerbrush faded into the distance, she realized she wasn't leaving anything behind. She was carrying it with her. And she was moving forward.

EPILOGUE

The meadow behind the Puckerbrush Community Center stretched wide and green under the golden glow of the late spring afternoon. Wildflowers swayed gently in the breeze, their colors vivid against the backdrop of the green fields, while the soft hum of conversation floated through the air.

The chairs were arranged in neat rows, draped in white linen, and tied with sprigs of lavender and baby's breath. The arch at the front was simple yet elegant, twined with ivy and more of the delicate blooms that seemed to grow wild in this little corner of the world.

It was the perfect place. The only place.

Constantine stood just inside the Community Center, her fingers trembling slightly as she adjusted the lace sleeves of her wedding dress. Abigail stood beside her, her calm, steady presence grounding her as she straightened the hem of Constantine's veil.

"You're beautiful," Abigail said, her eyes shimmering with unshed tears.

Constantine let out a nervous laugh, brushing her hands down the smooth fabric of her gown. "I feel like I might trip halfway down the aisle."

Abigail smiled, tucking a stray curl behind Constantine's ear. "If you do, Thomas will catch you. He's been waiting for this moment as long as you have."

Constantine's breath hitched, the warmth of Abigail's words settling over her. She turned toward the window, her gaze falling on the scene outside.

The guests were settling into their seats, laughter, and conversation mingling as the small town she loved gathered to witness this new chapter in her life.

Martha and Charles sat in the front row, Charles's arm resting protectively around her shoulders. Berta chatted animatedly with Emily, her vibrant voice carrying above the hum of the crowd. John stood near the refreshment table with Parker perched on his shoulders, the boy's laughter ringing clearly as he tugged at his father's hair.

Samuel Piper and Lydia sat a few rows back, their baby cradled in Lydia's arms as she whispered something that made Piper's smile stretch wide. Penelope sat next to Lydia, smiling proudly.

And there, just beside the arch, stood Thomas.

He looked impossibly handsome in his tailored suit, his hair catching the light as he shifted slightly, his hands clasped in front of him. But it was the look on his face that stole Constantine's breath. The quiet awe, the unshakable certainty, the love radiating from him as though she was the only thing in the world that mattered.

"You ready?" Abigail asked gently, her voice pulling Constantine back to the moment.

Constantine nodded, her fingers tightening briefly around the bouquet of wildflowers in her hands. "I've never been more ready for anything in my life."

Abigail smiled, stepping back as the music played, the soft strains of a violin carrying through the open air. Constantine took a deep breath, her heart pounding as she stepped outside, the sunlight warming her skin as every pair of eyes turned toward her.

But she only saw him.

Thomas's expression shifted as she walked down the aisle, his eyes glistening with emotion. He didn't look away, didn't blink, as though he were memorizing every detail of this moment.

When she reached him, the world seemed to quiet, the hum of the crowd and the music fading into the background.

"You look beautiful," he whispered, his voice rough with feeling as he took her hand.

Constantine smiled, the fear in her chest replaced by something brighter, something boundless. "You look very handsome," she whispered back.

The ceremony was simple, heartfelt, filled with quiet laughter and more than a few tears. Abigail and Matthew stood together as witnesses, their children, Archer and Grace, perched beside them with wide, curious eyes.

Emily dabbed at her tears with a handkerchief, nudging John when Parker tried to slip away toward the wildflowers. Berta held her hands clasped tightly, nodding emphatically at every word spoken, while Martha and Charles shared a soft smile, their hands entwined in their laps.

When the vows were spoken, and the kiss sealed their promise, the small crowd erupted into cheers, the sound carrying out over the hills to where a small oak tree shaded two simple stones, each carved with names that had shaped their journey:

Eldon Carter

"In quiet remembrance, we find peace."

Edward Dalton

"The past speaks not to chain us, but to guide us forward."

Hours before the ceremony, Constantine had knelt, her fingers brushing lightly over Eldon's name. For years, his choices had been a weight she carried, his guilt woven into her identity. But now, the guilt felt softer, less heavy.

Thomas stood beside her, his hand settling on her shoulder. "They'll always be a part of us," he breathed. "But they don't define us. That's something we get to decide."

She nodded, her chest swelling with gratitude as she placed a small bundle of lavender and rosemary at the base of Eldon's stone.

Thomas did the same for Edward's, the gesture simple but deeply felt.

"Thank you," Constantine whispered, her voice steady as the wind stirred softly around them.

Thomas held out his hand, his smile gentle. "Shall we?"

She took it, glancing over her shoulder one last time as they walked back across the meadow. The stones rested quietly beneath the oak tree, not forgotten but no longer a burden.

Much later, as the sun dipped lower, painting the sky in streaks of amber and rose, Constantine stood at the edge of the celebration, watching Thomas lean down to speak with Parker, his face lighting up when the boy laughed and tugged on his tie.

Abigail appeared beside her, a glass of champagne in hand. "You did it," she said, her eyes sparkling with pride.

"We did," Constantine replied with certainty.

Abigail smiled, her gaze following Constantine's. "So, where's the honeymoon?"

Her smile widened, her heart lifting. "Italy. We leave in two days."

"Rome?"

"And Florence," Constantine added. "And some tiny coastal towns where we can just... wander."

Raising her glass, Abigail said, "That sounds perfect."

"It will be," Constantine said, her gaze finding Thomas across the meadow.

He caught her eye, his smile wide and unguarded, and she felt it in every part of her. This was her beginning. Their beginning.

And it was everything she had ever needed.

ACKNOWLEDGMENTS

Dear Readers,

As I write this letter, my heart is filled with gratitude, nostalgia, and a bittersweet sense of farewell. Thank you for joining me on this journey through Puckerbrush, for embracing its quirks, its heartaches, its triumphs, and most importantly, its people. Your love for this series has been overwhelming, and it means the world to me.

When I first started this series, the characters were already with me, whispering their stories, sharing their struggles, and making me laugh with their stubbornness and humor. They've been more than fictional creations; they've become family. Abigail's wisdom, Berta's spirit, Constantine's courage, and Thomas's steady heart. Matthew, with his unwavering loyalty and love for Abigail and his family. On the other hand, Piper brought an understated charm and depth with his gentle but determined nature, revealing that strength can be found in kindness and quiet conviction. Together, they added layers of warmth that shaped this series in ways I will always treasure. Each of these characters holds a special place in my life. I've lived with them for so long that saying goodbye feels a little like packing up and leaving my favorite home.

And yet, I know that Puckerbrush will always be here. For me. For you. For anyone who needs to return to its green fields, its quiet streets, and its vibrant, flawed, loving people. I'll miss writing their stories, but I'll revisit them the same way I hope you will by reading the words that brought them to life.

This series has been a labor of love, but I couldn't have brought it to life without the help of a few amazing people. My heartfelt thanks go to **Lynne Pearson** of **All That Editing** for keeping me on track, ensuring timelines flowed smoothly, names stayed consistent, and details never got lost in the shuffle. Your expertise and guidance have been invaluable, Lynne, and I am so grateful to have had you by my side throughout this journey.

I also want to thank **Rebecca Sterling** for her stunning cover designs. All I had to do was tell Rebecca about the story, and her artistic vision brought Puckerbrush to life in ways I never could have imagined. Her work has been instrumental in sharing the heart of these stories with readers even before they turned the first page.

And, of course, to you, my readers. Thank you for embracing Puckerbrush with open arms. Your messages, reviews, and kind words about this little town and its people have brought me more joy than I could ever express. You've helped me bring Puckerbrush to life, and I am endlessly grateful for that.

As I close this chapter, I invite you to return to Puckerbrush whenever you like. Pull up a chair at the Puckerbrush Café, catch up with Berta's latest gossip, or walk the quiet fields where secrets linger and love blooms. I'll be there too, from time to time, because some places and some people are simply too dear to leave behind forever.

From the bottom of my heart, thank you for letting me share this journey with you.

With love and gratitude,

C. Deanne Rowe

ABOUT THE AUTHOR

C. Deanne Rowe was born and raised in southwest Oklahoma. She has also lived in Nebraska, Texas, and California. Iowa has been her home for over thirty years where she lives with her husband, two children and their spouses, five grandchildren, the memory of her hero teacup toy poodle, Allie, and her new rescue French Bulldog, Kendell

Learn more about C. Deanne Rowe, her books, sign up for her newsletter, and receive a free ebook at:

www.cdeannerowe.com

ALSO BY C. DEANNE ROWE

Valley Series:

In The Heart of Valley

Return to Valley

Dream of Valley

Puckerbrush Series:

Secrets of Puckerbrush

Return to Puckerbrush

Beyond Puckerbrush

Christmas In Puckerbrush

Last Revival in Puckerbrush

Cowboy Temptation Series:

Colt and Cassy

Southern Sophistication

Cowboy Owns Her Heart

Accidental Cowgirl Alana's List

Remember Me

Miller Canyon Ranch Series:

Bread, Beignets, and Cowboy Boots

The Family Tree

Through My Eyes

After A Broken Heart

Just One Kiss

Shattered Walls Series:

Shattered Walls

Shattered Connections

www.ingramcontent.com/pod-product-compliance
Lightning Source LLC
Chambersburg PA
CBHW071515170626
46811CB00007B/2867